AF515892

The Mystery Of The Train

Reprinting Edition

June 8 2025

July 12 2025

August 9 2025

September 17 2025

Latest printing Edition – September 17, 2025

Edited by Alden Dalmet

Cover page designed by Elisn Alphanso

The Mystery Of The Train

CHARACTERS

Name	Age
1. Nilen	13
2. Theo	13
3. Peter	24
4. Caleb	22
5. Emily	21
6. Harry	22
7. Dacy	20
8. Lucan	58
9. Max	26
10. Damien	26
11. Celia	17
12. Alex	19
13. Anika	15
14. Dilen	25
15. Anil	38

Introduction

The Mystery of Train No. 00331 presents a haunting and thought-provoking expedition into the unknown.

Set against the rhythmic sound of railway tracks and the soft illumination of vintage train compartments, these narrative invites readers to embark on a journey unlike any other—where time becomes irrelevant, and the mundane shifts into the remarkable.

In a realm where the lines of reality become indistinct, a group of young adventurers boards a train that defies existence.

What starts as an ordinary trip quickly evolves into a voyage into something far more profound—a domain where bizarre coincidences, unsettling silence, and shadowy recollections linger just out of sight.

The number on the locomotive may read 00331, but the route it takes is anything but conventional.

With every mile that passes, whispers intensify, time elongates and contracts, and inquiries abound.

What is genuine? What is a figment of imagination?

And what narratives lie concealed within the train's tattered seats, its flickering lights, and its unvoiced stillness?

The characters must confront not only what awaits them but also the echoes of what may have been abandoned.

A story of bravery, connection, and subtle dread, this Book delves into the emotional terrains of youth, memory, and ambiguity.

It offers no guarantees of answers, only the resonance of questions posed in the darkness. So, step aboard. Take a look around.

The adventure is commencing. And some destinations remain uncharted on any map.

Book Guide

Before each chapter, there is a scene description given on each chapter.

After the scene description, the story is given.

Kindly read the story and scene description for a better understanding of the chapter.

For Navigation through certain chapters, page numbers are given.

If anything is unclear, please let me know at my email.

aldendalmet@gmail.com

aldendalmet331@gmail.com

Content

pages

The Mystery Of The Train

About The Author

The author of the book “The Mystery Of The Train” is Alden Sunil Dalmet, a 14-year-old author who studies at Notre Dame School, CBSE, located in Vasai Tarkhad. With a passion for creativity and a flair for writing stories. Alden began his writing journey at the young age of 11 and completed his debut Book, "The Mystery of the Train 00331," by the age of 12.

Alden grew up in a supportive and loving family environment, where he was constantly inspired by the individuals surrounding him.

His mother, Mona Dalmet, and father, Sunil Dalmet, have been his main sources of motivation throughout his life. His sisters, Siona Dalmet and Adina Dalmet, also play important roles in his life. Furthermore, his maternal grandparents, Thomas Dabre and Carmel Dabre, along with his paternal grandparents, Mates Dalmet and Mary Dalmet, have had a profound impact on shaping his values, creativity, and determination.

The influence of his extended family, including his cousins, uncle, and aunt, has also contributed significantly to his personal development and outlook on life.

Writing is not just a hobby for Alden—it's a way of expressing the world he sees and the dreams he imagines. He enjoys crafting poems, writing meaningful quotes, and creating both short and long stories that stir emotions and curiosity.
This first book is a blend of suspense, mystery, and imagination, showing the depths of his storytelling skills at a young age.

Alden believes that encouragement at home and consistent dedication can turn any dream into reality. He wants his readers to know that age is never a barrier to creativity.

With each word he writes, he hopes to inspire his readers to follow their passion and believe in their unique gifts.

Everyone is unique in their work, with a focus and determination. Everything is possible.

Make your ideas, your creativity shine, and you'll see the success of your hard work with you.

Because if you think, you will!

Message to Readers:

Dear Readers,

I truly believe that imagination is the first step to creation. Writing this book has been one of the most exciting and challenging adventures of my life.

It started with a simple idea and turned into a full journey filled
with learning, emotion, and excitement. Every page of "Mystery of the Train 00331" carries a piece of my thoughts, my dreams and my hopes.

I want you to remember that no matter how young you are, or how big your dreams may seem, you have the power to achieve them.

All it takes is belief in yourself, patience to grow, and passion to push forward. I was just 11 when I started off with my book.

Through this story, I hope to spark a sense of wonder, courage, and mystery within you.

May it inspire you to chase your adventures—whether in writing, music, art, or anything that brings you joy. Never let fear of failure stop you.
The road may be tough, but the destination is always worth it.

Thank you for reading my work. I'm deeply grateful for your time, and I hope you enjoy every twist and turn in this story. This is just the beginning, and I promise there's much more to come.

With dreams and gratitude,
Alden Sunil Dalmet.

Author’s Disclaimer

This book is a complete work of fiction. Everything you read within its pages—including the characters, places, events, and dialogues—is born out of the author's imagination. If any similarities are found with real people, places, or incidents, it is purely coincidental and unintentional.

The story and its elements have been crafted with deep care and thoughtful creativity. The characters represent fictional lives and personalities created to serve the plot and message. Any interpretation connecting them to real people or identities is unintentional. The places, names, traditions, and environments used are imaginary unless otherwise mentioned.

The author respects all religions and does not target any of them.

The writing in this book is done with full respect to all human beings regardless of their caste, creed, religion, race, or gender. There is no intention to target, insult, or misrepresent any belief, culture, faith, institution, or social value. The story focuses on human emotions, values, and circumstances and should be taken as a piece of creative storytelling.

The author, being a young and developing writer, draws inspiration from various sources like books, films, daily life events, conversations, and creative thoughts. These inspirations are blended to create a unique and original story. There is no attempt to copy or misuse any original content of others. This book is a fresh creative expression from the author's own imagination.

This book is not a historical, political, or religious document. It does not intend to reflect any specific agenda or belief. The plot may include situations that deal with good and bad, truth and lies, victory and loss—but all of this is built only to convey moral messages, life values, and storytelling flow.

If at any point, any reader feels disturbed or misunderstood any portion of the content, the author kindly requests your understanding, and describe about the issue on aldendalmet@gmail.com. For more details, refer to the last page. Nothing has been written to offend. The author is committed to improving and learning as a writer and believes in inclusive, positive storytelling.

Fiction gives the freedom to create endless worlds—but with that freedom comes the responsibility of respect. This story was written with peace, love, and hope. It is meant to entertain, inspire, and make you think. The purpose is to leave the reader with meaningful thoughts, joy, and reflection.

Special care has been taken to avoid any form of negative impact or misrepresentation. Every piece of this story—from characters to plot points—has been handled with responsibility. The focus has always been on value-based storytelling, creativity, and inspiring imagination among young minds.

I, the author, believe that books are powerful tools to educate, heal, and uplift. They should bring people together, not divide them. Through this fictional journey, I hope to reach the hearts of readers with kindness, honesty, and creativity. Let us read with open minds and write with open hearts.

Thank you to every reader who has picked up this book and shown interest.

Your support encourages me to continue writing and growing. Please accept this disclaimer as a reflection of my sincerity and good intention. I welcome your suggestions, blessings, and feedback as I continue my writing path.

With great respect, care, and creativity,
Alden Sunil Dalmet

Special Thanks

I want to express my deepest and most heartfelt gratitude to everyone who has supported me on my journey of writing, learning, and growing as a person. This book and all my creative efforts would never have been possible without the love, guidance, and encouragement from those around me.

Each person mentioned here has played a unique and invaluable role in shaping who I am today.

First and foremost, I am eternally thankful to my family—the true foundation of my life. My mother, Mona Dalmet, and my father, Sunil Dalmet, have been my pillars of strength through every step of this journey.

Their unconditional love, patience, and belief in me have been my greatest motivation. When challenges seemed overwhelming, it was their words of encouragement that lifted me up and pushed me forward.

Their sacrifices and constant support have given me the freedom and confidence to pursue my dreams, and I will always be grateful for their unwavering faith in me.

My sisters, Siona Dalmet and Adina Dalmet, have been wonderful companions. Their kindness, playful encouragement, and genuine interest in my writing have made this process a joy. Sharing my thoughts and ideas with them has always sparked new inspiration, and their honest feedback has helped me become a better writer.

The joy we share as siblings has been a steady source of comfort and motivation during tough times.

I am profoundly thankful to my maternal grandparents, Thomas Dabre and Carmel, and my paternal grandparents, Mates Dalmet and Mary Dalmet.

Their wisdom, love, and life experiences have deeply influenced my values, creativity, and character. From them, I learned the importance of patience, hard work, and staying true to oneself.

Their stories and lessons have enriched my perspective beyond what books could teach, and their unwavering support has been a guiding light in my life.

My extended family—cousins, uncle, and aunt—have also played a vital role in my development. Their encouragement and warmth remind me that I am never alone on this path.

Family gatherings filled with laughter and shared stories have fueled my imagination and reminded me of the importance of community.

I am grateful to have such a loving and supportive network.

I would like to sincerely thank my school, Notre Dame School, and especially our principal and all my teachers. Their dedication to nurturing my talents and helping me improve my weaknesses has been invaluable.

They saw potential in me even when I doubted myself and patiently guided me towards excellence.

The knowledge, discipline, and encouragement I received at school created a strong foundation for my growth, both academically and personally.

My friends have been an essential part of this journey as well. Their friendship, encouragement, and honest feedback kept me motivated and joyful throughout the writing process.

Whether it was sharing ideas, helping me stay focused, or simply offering a smile when I needed it most, they have been a constant source of strength.

I am truly lucky to have such supportive and inspiring friends.

Special thanks to Fr. Tony D'Souza and Fr. Jokim Fernandes, whose expert consulting helped me navigate challenges during my writing.

Fr. Joseph D'Souza's guidance was a source of wisdom and encouragement, keeping me focused and motivated. Fr. Savio D'Monte dedicated his time to proofreading my manuscript.

Their mentorship has enriched this book and helped me grow as a writer and as a person.

Above all, I am deeply grateful to God. His blessings, guidance, and grace have been my foundation throughout this journey.

In moments of doubt and difficulty, His presence gave me strength, hope, and courage. This book is a testament to His endless mercy and love, and I thank Him for every opportunity and success.

Finally, I extend my warmest thanks to everyone who believed in me—my schoolmates, family friends, classmates, and all the kind souls who cheered me on from near and far.

Your faith in me inspired me to keep dreaming big. Knowing that so many people supported me made all the difference and reminded me that no dream is too big with love and encouragement.

This journey has been one of the most beautiful and rewarding experiences of my life.

I carry the support, kindness, and encouragement of all these incredible people in my heart as I continue to grow as a writer and as a person.

Thank you for being a part of my story and for inspiring me to reach for the stars.

Thank You!

Dedication letter

This book is dedicated with all my heart to those who made this dream possible, those who believed in me, and those who stood by me as I took my first step into the world of storytelling .

To my parents, thank you for being the pillars of my life. Your love is the reason I am who I am today. You both taught me how to dream and how to work hard to make those dreams come true.

You reminded me every day that even when I'm young, I can still make a difference in the world. Your encouragement gave me strength on the days when I didn't believe in myself.

Every word I've written carries the spirit of the values you've instilled in me. This book is a reflection of your love and support.

To my grandparents, thank you for your wisdom, stories, and blessings. Your lives have been my greatest inspiration.

You've taught me patience, kindness, and humility, and those lessons live in the pages of this book. Your prayers and faith in me have meant more than words can express.

To my school – Notre Dame School, Vasai, my teachers, my principal, and everyone who guided me, thank you for nurturing my talent and correcting my mistakes with kindness.

You've given me a foundation that will last a lifetime. To Fr. Tony D'Souza, Fr. Joseph D'Souza, Fr. Jokim Fernandes, and Fr. Savio D'Monte, your guidance, your listening ears, and your willingness to help have made this path so much brighter.

Your belief in this project helped me believe in it, too. Thank you for offering your time and wisdom to shape this book with love and care.

To God, who is the ultimate Author of my life, thank you for giving me the gift of imagination and the courage to use it. Without Your grace and blessings, I would not have been able to complete this Book.

You gave me the strength to begin, the courage to keep going, and the joy of finishing it. This book is for Your glory and the dreams You planted in my heart.

And lastly, to everyone who has read this book, supported my writing, or simply shared a kind word, you have touched my life in ways you may never know.

This book is a result of love, support, prayer, and encouragement. It is a piece of my soul, and I offer it to you with immense gratitude.

From the bottom of my heart—
Thank you.

With love and dedication,
Alden Sunil Dalmet
(Author of *Mystery of the Train 00331*

Character introduction

Nilen

Nilen, a 13-year-old boy, is the heart of the group. Adventurous and curious, he is the first to act when something seems unusual.

His quick thinking and natural leadership qualities make him someone the others look up to, even during the most unsettling moments.

Nilen's strength lies in his bravery and instincts. He is deeply observant, has a knack for finding clues, and takes initiative when the team needs direction.

His strong moral compass and unshakeable loyalty to his friends push him to protect and help others even when afraid.

However, Nilen can sometimes be impulsive and act before fully considering the consequences.

He occasionally lets fear drive his decisions, which can lead to risky situations.

But his ability to learn from his mistakes makes him grow with every challenge the team faces.

Theo

Theo is Nilen’s close friend, also 13 years old. He is witty and intelligent, often offering creative and out-of-the-box solutions.

Though not as outspoken, Theo is observant and deeply empathetic, sensing when his friends need support.

His strengths include a sharp memory and quick analytical skills.

Theo is also very calm under pressure and often helps balance Nilen's impulsive nature with rational thinking.

Theo’s weaknesses include a tendency to doubt himself and second-guess his decisions.

In high-stress situations, he may retreat emotionally, but his loyalty always brings him back to support his friends.

Peter

Peter, a 24-year-old, is the elder figure in the group and often plays the role of the protector.

He brings maturity and a calm demeanor to chaotic situations.

His experience and logical mind make him a natural at organizing plans and solving puzzles.

Peter's greatest strength is his composure under pressure. He is a strong communicator, often mediating conflicts among the group and maintaining focus during investigations.

Despite his strengths, Peter sometimes distances himself emotionally.

His serious nature may make him seem cold or detached, but his actions reveal a deep sense of care for everyone.

Caleb

Caleb, aged 22, is energetic, enthusiastic, and a quick learner.

He believes in action over talk and is always ready to face danger head-on. He respects logic and is practical in his approach to mysteries.

His key strengths are adaptability and courage. Caleb often volunteers to take on the more physically demanding tasks and never hesitates to protect others.

However, his directness can come off as insensitive at times.

He struggles to express emotions, which can create misunderstandings among his peers, but his intentions are always pure.

Emily

Emily, 21, is gentle, thoughtful, and deeply compassionate. She has an intuitive understanding of people and is the emotional anchor of the group.

Emily is excellent at reading body language and emotions, making her invaluable during interrogations or tense moments.

Her strengths lie in her empathy, patience, and insight.

She often brings a new perspective that others may overlook and helps soothe conflicts in the group.

Emily's biggest challenge is her tendency to become emotionally overwhelmed.

She can sometimes carry the burdens of others too deeply, which affects her ability to make objective decisions.

Harry

Harry, 22, is a steady and confident presence. He's practical and often acts as the realist in the group.

While others may get swept away by fear or excitement, Harry stays grounded and reminds everyone to think clearly.

He's strong-willed and reliable, known for his sense of direction and attention to detail. When others panic, Harry remains firm, making him a dependable leader in high-stress situations.

Harry sometimes struggles with flexibility; he prefers plans and dislikes unpredictability.

This can lead to conflicts in spontaneous moments, but he's learning to adapt through their shared experiences.

Dacy

Dacy, at 20 years old, is the group's intellectual powerhouse.

She is methodical, scientific, and always seeks logical explanations before jumping to conclusions.

She's particularly skilled at deciphering puzzles and solving complex problems.

Her strengths include rational thinking, research skills, and strategic planning. Dacy is often the one who connects the dots between multiple clues.

Her reliance on facts can make her skeptical of anything supernatural or emotional, which sometimes clashes with other members' beliefs.

She struggles to deal with intuition-based decisions.

Lucan

Lucan, the 58-year-old train engineer, is a mysterious figure whose knowledge of the train holds many secrets. He is wise, experienced, and carries a deep understanding of the supernatural elements tied to the train.

His strength lies in his knowledge and historical understanding of the train's origins.

He is respectful, patient, and generous with his insights when he chooses to share them.

However, Lucan tends to withhold information and speak in riddles, which frustrates the group.

His reluctance to fully explain his past creates tension, though he usually reveals vital truths at the right moment.

Max

Max, a 26-year-old from the United States, is the tech-savvy member of the group.

Calm and methodical, he often acts as the investigator behind the scenes, decoding messages, unlocking devices, and analyzing digital clues.

His logical mindset complements the team's more intuitive members.

His strength lies in his technical knowledge and critical thinking.

Whether it's bypassing a locked phone or tracking down a lead from a photograph, Max provides tools and insights others can't.

He's dependable, especially during digital investigations.

Max can, however, come across as emotionally detached. He sometimes prioritizes evidence over human emotions, which can create distance between him and others.

Despite this, he values the group and proves his loyalty through actions rather than words.

Damien

Damien, also 26 and Max's close friend, is adaptable, resourceful, and empathetic. His laid-back demeanor helps balance the tension when emotions run high. Damien has a knack for calming others and grounding the group in logic and reality.

His strength is his emotional intelligence—he reads people well and offers advice when it's most needed. He is also creative in problem-solving and knows how to lift the group's spirits even during the darkest moments.

Damien's weakness is that he can be overly trusting. His desire to see the good in others sometimes clouds his judgment, putting him and the group at risk. However, his willingness to learn from his experiences helps him mature quickly through the story.

Celia

Celia, a determined 17-year-old, is smart, assertive, and doesn't hesitate to speak her mind. She's highly organized and often acts as the planner when the group needs to coordinate their efforts across time and place.

Her greatest strengths are her leadership skills and decisiveness. Celia is not easily swayed by fear and is known for making bold calls when others hesitate. She thrives in investigative settings and keeps the group focused.

Her main weakness is her stubbornness. Celia tends to hold strong opinions and can be slow to admit when she's wrong. This can cause friction, but she is deeply loyal and committed to the mission and her friends.

Alex

Alex, 19 years old, is the documentarian of the group. He keeps track of every clue, writes everything down, and ensures that details aren't lost in the chaos. Quiet and observant, Alex often notices patterns others miss.

His strengths are memory, note-taking, and analytical thinking. Alex is vital in organizing the story's timeline and piecing together fragmented clues into a meaningful picture.

Despite his intellect, Alex struggles with self-doubt. He sometimes feels overlooked and lacks confidence to speak up, even when he has key insights. Over time, he finds his voice and realizes his importance to the team.

Anika

Anika, just 15, is wise beyond her years. She's intuitive and imaginative, often sensing things that others dismiss. Anika brings a fresh, creative outlook to the group's investigations and is sensitive to the emotional atmosphere around her.

Her strengths include emotional insight and lateral thinking. She often picks up on minor, hidden clues—like tone of voice, a forgotten object, or a shift in someone's story—that others overlook.

Anika's youth means she can be underestimated, and she sometimes feels left out of major decisions. Her sensitivity also makes her vulnerable to fear and doubt, but her courage grows as she proves herself again and again.

Dilen

Dilen, 25 years old, is the quiet observer of the group. He doesn't speak much, but when he does, his words carry weight. Emotionally complex and deeply connected to his past, Dilen's personal journey intertwines with the mystery at hand.

His strengths are his intuition and strong emotional resilience. Dilen remains calm under pressure and is willing to make sacrifices for the greater good, showing depth of character that inspires the group.

However, Dilen carries emotional baggage that can cloud his focus. Memories of his past and personal losses weigh heavily on him, making him vulnerable to emotional decisions. Yet his heart remains his strongest guide.

Anil

Anil, a 38-year-old from Kolkata, is the oldest in the main group. He initially boards the train by accident but quickly becomes a vital member of the team. With his life experience, he brings practical knowledge and street-smart thinking.

His strengths are reliability, maturity, and calmness in tense moments. Anil is someone the younger members respect. He often thinks a few steps ahead and helps keep the team grounded when the supernatural elements grow overwhelming.

Anil's weakness is his hesitation to trust others quickly. Having seen betrayal in the past, he tends to keep his guard up. This occasionally causes friction, but his actions consistently prove his commitment to solving the mystery and protecting the group.

1

Misunderstanding of the train

The night was a heavy blanket of darkness, the kind that swallowed every sound and movement. Above the deserted platform, a few pale yellow lamps flickered, their glow trembling against the stubborn chill in the air.

The wind dragged along the smell of metal and rain, whispering through the overhead wires like a secret.

Far beyond the station's edge, the rails stretched into the void, glinting faintly under the moonlight before vanishing into blackness.

The team stood scattered, each figure a shadow among shadows, their breaths forming small clouds that dissolved into the cold.

Shoes scraped faintly against the worn concrete, a quiet rhythm in the vast stillness. Somewhere in the distance, a loose tin sheet rattled, its sharp clinks echoing longer than they should have.

The station clock ticked lazily, its hands stubbornly creeping toward midnight.

The air carried the metallic tang of the rails mixed with the faint aroma of burnt coal—remnants of trains long gone.

Each sound, each shadow felt magnified here, as though the station itself was holding its breath, waiting for something to arrive.

Somewhere deep in the silence, the faintest hum began—a vibration so soft it might have been imagined.

Yet it lingered, low and steady, pulsing in the bones, carrying with it the strange certainty that the night was far from ordinary.

The mystery of train no. 00331

What a traveling day! We had fun these days with our uncle, said Nilen. Yes, but although we had fun, we missed our family too.

Suddenly, a train stopped and prepared to depart.

"That train appears quite old and antiquated, having been in service for decades, does it not?" inquired Alex.

Is that our train? The number matches, 00331," Theo questioned. "No, wait! Our train is actually 00311," Anika corrected him. "But does it really matter? Both trains are headed to Amritsar, and besides, it is getting late, and our train has yet to arrive," illegal to step in other train, the ticket checker can even charge us for that.

2

Meeting Damien and Max

The train's interior swayed gently, a soft, almost hypnotic motion that made the shadows dance along the walls. Dim yellow bulbs buzzed faintly overhead, casting pools of weak light that barely reached the corners of the carriage. The seats, worn and faded, bore the marks of countless journeys—creases, stains, and small tears that whispered of years gone by.

The faint scent of old fabric mingled with the sharper tang of machine oil, seeping from the joints and gears hidden beneath the floor.

The windows, streaked with dust and raindrops, reflected distorted shapes—faces, coats, and silhouettes—that seemed to move even when no one stirred. Beyond them, the outside world was little more than a shifting blur of black and grey, with the occasional flash of a distant signal light flaring briefly like a watchful eye.

Somewhere in the distance, the hollow metallic groan of the wheels deepened, echoing through the carriage like a slow heartbeat.

A stillness hung over the place, the kind that presses against the eardrums and makes every small sound—every creak of the wood, every faint sigh of air—seem unnaturally loud.

Yet beneath that sound, there was something else—a more irregular note, like the subtle shift of weight somewhere unseen, or the whisper of movement just beyond the reach of the light.

The narrow aisle between the seats stretched ahead, half-lit, as though daring anyone to walk its length.

The sense was inescapable: the train was in motion, but not all of it was mechanical. Something else seemed to be traveling along with it.

A boy's sudden scream pierced the stillness of the night, prompting us to rush towards him.

Upon arriving, we discovered that we were the only passengers on the train, yet we diligently searched for the boy, to no avail.

The clock read 2:30 AM.

While we continued our search, we heard noises emanating from a nearby area.

Investigating further, we encountered two individuals who appeared to be looking for something.

Curiosity piqued, we inquired about their search. Alex asked, "What are you looking for?" They responded, "We heard a scream, so we came here.

" As they spoke, the train began to move, and fortunately, their luggage remained with them, although the ticket checker was absent. Feeling fatigued, we took a seat and introduced ourselves: "My name is Nilen, this is Theo, Anika, Celia, and Alex, and we are from Amritsar."

The two men introduced themselves as Max and Damien, hailing from New Mexico, United States.

Suddenly, the train accelerated, reaching an approximate speed of 250 km/h. We momentarily disregarded this and continued our conversation. At 3:15 AM, an unexpected announcement echoed through the carriage: "Next station, Amritsar, in two hours."

Shortly thereafter, a woman's piercing scream filled the air, causing discomfort in our ears. We hurried towards the source of the sound, but, like before, we found nothing.

We speculated that it might be a time-triggered radio, yet there was no radio present.

The voice sounded distinctly real, instilling fear within us. We decided to sit quietly for a while.

At 4:05 AM, we were startled by the sound of footsteps approaching us.

Fear gripped us as the figure drew nearer, heightening our anxiety.

3

Meeting Anil

A thin ribbon of mist clung stubbornly to the carriage floor, curling and shifting as the train swayed. The corridor ahead was narrow, its walls close enough that every movement brushed a shoulder against cool metal.

The air was still, as if the ventilation had stopped, heavy with the faint scent of rust and aged wood polish. Overhead, a single light flickered, buzzing faintly before casting the hall back into half-shadow, making every shadow seem to twitch and stretch along the walls.

The windows here were smaller, boxed in by metal frames that had dulled to a tired brown over the years.

Beyond them, only darkness rolled past, interrupted by the fleeting glint of rail-side posts and the occasional spark from the overhead wires.

Each flash revealed just enough to remind anyone looking out that the world beyond was rushing by, unseen and unknowable.

Somewhere behind, the low hum of the engine seemed to falter for a moment before resuming, steady but… different.

It was as though the train had taken a breath. The air in the corridor shifted ever so slightly, carrying a whisper of colder wind from nowhere in particular. The faint creak of floorboards underfoot betrayed movement—though it was impossible to tell whether it came from the next carriage or from somewhere unseen within the shadows themselves.

The door at the far end of the corridor loomed like a silent guardian, its glass opaque with years of scratches and dust.

A faint smear—something dark—streaked across one side, as if someone had brushed it in haste. The silence here wasn't empty; it was watchful, filled with the kind of pause that makes the skin tighten at the back of the neck.

Even without seeing another soul, the feeling was clear: no one in this part of the train was truly alone.

A sudden interruption occurred when someone opened the compartment door, and a man entered, inquiring, "Have you heard a scream?

" He explained, "I followed the sound and ended up here." Celia responded, "No, we have searched for her everywhere but found no trace." Alex then asked,

"By the way, what is your name?" The man replied, "My name is Anil, and I am from Kolkata, West Bengal.

I boarded this train unknowingly after hearing a boy scream, so I came in to look for him.

However, I could not find him, and then the train door closed unexpectedly."

Anil continued, "I searched everywhere except for the motorman's cabin.

" Max noted, "That cabin is locked from the inside.

" Damien interjected, "I believe I can unlock it." Theo suggested, "Let us proceed to investigate that area."

Nilen asked, "Is this the motorman's cabin?" Anika confirmed, "Yes, I think it is."

After opening the door and entering, they found the cabin empty. Celia questioned, "Then who is operating the train?

" Damien then observed, "It appears to be on autopilot mode; look over there. Since there is nothing here, let us leave."

Suddenly, Anika pointed out, "Wait! Look at this seat; it seems like something, a kind of… a red liquid like blood ." Anil added, "Yes, it is frightening; it seems someone may have been killed here. We should take a picture." Max urged, "Now, let us exit this place."

At that moment, Alex received a notification indicating that the train was delayed by five hours.

At 5:13 AM, an unexpectedly loud sound echoed through the train, irritating us.

Suddenly, the lights flickered before plunging the train into complete darkness.

Unable to see anything, Max and Damien grabbed a torch, but the glass of the filament shattered, reminiscent of paranormal occurrences.

We were petrified.

4

The train reaches Amritsar

The train slid into the station with a muted screech of steel, its motion slowing until the carriages shuddered to a halt.

Outside, the pale light of early dawn clung to the world like a thin veil, revealing just enough to hint at shapes and shadows. The air hung heavy with the scent of damp stone, wet earth, and the faint, lingering tang of coal smoke.

The platform stretched into the mist, its cracked tiles glistening faintly from the night's rain.

A few iron benches, slick with moisture, sat empty under tall lamps whose glow was dulled by the fog. Every sound here seemed softened—muffled footsteps, the faint hiss of steam escaping from under the train, and the low groan of settling metal.

Beyond the platform's edge, the station building rose like a quiet sentinel, its faded walls stained with the memory of countless seasons.

A single clock, its glass slightly fogged, ticked steadily, the movement almost hypnotic in the hushed air. Somewhere in the rafters, unseen pigeons stirred, their coos and the flutter of wings echoing softly overhead.

In the distance, a bell clanged once—sharp and unexpected—then fell silent again, leaving behind only the whisper of the mist curling along the tracks.

The rails themselves gleamed faintly, vanishing into the fog in both directions, as if the station were cut off from the rest of the world.

The stillness was the kind that felt unnatural, as though the place had been paused in time. Even the fog seemed reluctant to move, clinging stubbornly to every edge and corner.

Standing there, surrounded by the quiet and the pale light, it was easy to believe that the station had been waiting—not for the morning, but for something, or someone, yet to arrive.

At that moment, the train finally arrived in Amritsar, accompanied by an announcement declaring "destination Amritsar.

" We swiftly gathered our luggage and exited the train. However, Nilen, while making his way out, discovered something.

Given the urgency of the situation, he placed it in his bag and hurried outside.

Once we were off the train, Nilen exclaimed, "I found something! Wait, look at this; it's a small bag."

"Yes, I believe so," he added. Alex urged, "Check what's inside."

"I am checking it now; look here," Nilen replied. Inside, we found some money, a small diary, a wallet, and a phone.

"Show me the phone," Anika requested.

After examining the phone for a few moments, Anika exclaimed, "What! Look at this; it displays the wrong date—December 2007, while this phone indicates December 2017."

To verify, we asked others around us, and to our astonishment, everyone confirmed it was indeed December 17, 2017.

We were incredulous; how could this be

To confirm it we asked the other people and we were astonished that the people whom we asked all answered on 17 December 2017.

Stop wasting time and let's hurry home said Theo. Damien and I will search for a taxi but where should we stay? Said Max, so you stay with us said Celia.

(after some time)

(after reaching home)

It looks so old isn't it said Nilen yes, so can I go home now said Anil. How can it be we should investigate this problem shall we, yes, I think my mother is waiting for me said Anil ok but give me your number said Alex my number is

(+91 123xxxxxxx) and I will be available anytime on this number okay so well bye see you later.

Where are our parents? said Anika, well nobody knows said Celia.

But see the tree it is ravaged I think there was a cyclone during the period between 2007 and 2017 said Damien yes, I think so.

Wait we forgot about our grandmother said Theo, yes, we forgot about it said Nilen, so let's go inside.

(going inside)

We were shocked that there was nobody inside the house we searched everywhere but we couldn't find our grandmother.

As we were going outside,

Suddenly Nilen saw his grandmother's photo frame hanging to the wall beside the window he interrupted;

Isn't that our grandmother's picture, yes, it is but why is it hanging, is our grandmother dead said Theo I think so said Alex.

Then we went outside the house and saw our neighbors who were exercising we asked them about our grandmother,

They were astonished to see us as they had not seen us for a decade.

They asked;

Where were you all? We thought that you all were dead and where have you been, said curiously, we had gone on 2nd December 2007.

Departure was on 27th December 2007 as we stepped on the train, the train started.

Still, on the way it speeded up like 300 km/h, suddenly I got a message that our train was delayed for something like 2 hours (approx.) and after some hours as it reached the station but during traveling on that train, we heard strange sounds, screams which made us scared.

But how did our grandmother die said Celia, she died because when she had no news she became sad but did not lose hope but one night that was on 21st March 2013 she died and ever since then we used to clean this house monthly because she told us, but before that, she left a message hoping you would come, so where's that message I don't know.

Don't tell anyone that we are here that's a secret, till we investigate this issue, said Alex.

Okay fine.

5

Mission investigation.

Morning crept into the room slowly, spilling through thin curtains in muted gold. The sunlight, softened by the lingering mist outside, settled across the wooden floor in long, slanted lines, catching on motes of dust that drifted lazily through the air.

The faint scent of tea leaves and warm bread mingled with the sharper tang of metal from somewhere beyond the walls—a quiet reminder that the train tracks were never far away.

The table in the center bore the marks of age, its surface scratched and burnished by years of use. A half-folded newspaper lay on one corner, its pages curling slightly from the dampness in the air.

Somewhere in the distance, a kettle hissed softly before releasing a brief, tired whistle. The sound seemed almost too loud in the otherwise muted space.

Outside, the world was just beginning to stir. The faint murmur of voices reached through the thin walls—muffled, indistinct—punctuated by the occasional clink of cups or the low creak of a door opening and closing.

The air was cool enough to carry the crisp scent of dew, and every so often, a soft breeze would slip in, rustling the edge of the curtains.

The ticking of a clock on the far wall kept time with the quiet rhythm of the morning, each second stretching just a little too long.

The stillness had a weight to it, not oppressive, but watchful—like the moment before a conversation that will change everything.

In that pause between the day beginning and the world fully waking, there was an odd sense of expectation, as if the room, the street beyond, and the very air itself knew that something was about to happen—and was simply waiting for it to arrive.

As dawn broke, the remnants of the previous night's unsettling dream lingered in our minds, casting a shadow over the day ahead.

The sun's rays filtered through the curtains, and the aroma of breakfast wafted through the air, beckoning us to the dining table.

We gathered, albeit with a sense of unease, each of us lost in our thoughts about the investigation and the haunting images from our dreams.

Let us commence with breakfast, followed by a brief rest, after which we will strategize for the investigation.

However, we must determine a suitable location for our discussion. The study room will serve as our meeting place.

We shall convene promptly at 9:00 AM, and please remember to inform Anil about this arrangement.

At 9:00 AM, Celia inquired, "Is everyone present?" She then paused, "But where is Anil? He has not arrived yet."

"I am here! I am here!" came Anil's response.

Now, let us initiate the investigation.

1. The train number is 00331.

2. The following clues have been identified:

a. A mobile phone

b. A diary

c. A wallet, which was wrapped in a newspaper

d. Some cash:

- 3 notes of 100
- 5 notes of 50
- 7 notes of 10
- 2 notes of 5

e. A small bag

Total amount: ₹ 630

3. There were screams from a boy and a woman.

4. The approximate time was 2:15.

5. There is a ten-year gap from 2007 to 2017.

"I have a clue," I stated. "I enjoy taking selfies and photographs, and I captured some images on the train. I also have a camera with me."

Thus, we have:

6. Photos and images on the phones

7. Videos on the camera

"Is this situation related to mathematical calculations?" Theo asked. "I do not believe so," Max replied.

"If we travel on this train again, we might find ourselves in 2027," Damien suggested. "I think that logic is flawed," he added.

"However, we require additional clues," Anika remarked.

"Are there any other points to discuss?" Anil responded, "No, I believe that is sufficient.

We will reconvene tomorrow at 11:00 AM, so please reflect on this matter until then."

Later that night, at 2:00 AM, we were awakened by a terrifying nightmare.

We heard the screams of a boy and a woman, their faces and bodies obscured by blood-like structure, which was profoundly unsettling.

Upon waking, we initially dismissed it as just another nightmare, choosing to ignore it and return to sleep.

However, this was no ordinary dream; it recurred, growing louder

6

Discussion about the clues

The sun was higher now, but its warmth struggled to break through the veil of thin, drifting clouds. Outside the train window, the landscape stretched endlessly—a quilt of pale fields, scattered trees, and the occasional cluster of distant rooftops, their outlines softened by the morning haze.

The train cut through it all with a steady, rhythmic hum, its wheels singing faintly against the rails.

Inside the carriage, the air held a quiet restlessness. The seats, their fabric worn smooth by years of travel, whispered faint creaks with each sway of the train. A narrow strip of light slanted through the windows, tracing slow-moving patterns on the aisle floor as the train rocked gently.

The faint aroma of machine oil lingered beneath the sharper scent of brewed coffee drifting from somewhere down the corridor.

Every sound seemed amplified here: the low rattle of the windows in their frames, the metallic groan of the couplings between carriages, the occasional dull thud from overhead luggage shifting with the train's motion.

The hallway beyond the seats was empty, stretching toward the next carriage like a narrow passage between two worlds.

Outside, a lone bird kept pace for a few moments, its wings glinting briefly before it veered away into the open fields.

Shadows of telephone poles flashed rhythmically across the seats, marking the train's steady progress like a silent metronome.

The world beyond seemed peaceful enough, yet inside, the air carried a strange undercurrent—something not quite in harmony with the calm scenery.

The train moved on, but each mile felt less like a journey toward a destination and more like a slow crossing into the unknown, where the familiar rules of time and place had begun to quietly bend.

27th December 2017

Alex inquired if everyone had completed their reports. Upon receiving confirmation, he proceeded to review the findings, starting with the first item:

1. Phone ———————————— Max

In my assessment, the phone belongs to Surdesh Paten, a former glass company employee. He recorded a video during a train journey, narrating his experiences when suddenly a scream was heard, followed by gunfire, causing his phone to fall and the recording to cease. The device was secured with a PIN, which I managed to bypass through coding, revealing that the date associated with the phone was 17 December 1987. Surdesh had a sister and lost his father at a young age. He resided in Gujarat, having previously lived in Bhuj until a cyclone destroyed his home. Here is his photograph.

(looking at the photograph)

Now, let us move on to the next item:

2. Money ———————————— Alex

The total amount of money is RS 630 plus RS 285, which totals RS 915. The first bundle contained two notes, one marked with the number 76769 and the second with 89768. While these numbers may seem insignificant, the second bundle included a note stating, "I am Amal Asang and I need help," accompanied by bloodstains on the money. This suggests that he was in distress before his demise.

3. Pictures ——————— Damien and Nilen

Nilen: The photographs reveal two significant clues. The first clue is found in the second photo of the train, which appears to be quite old, while the seventh photo indicates it has been operational for the past two years.

Damien: This implies that it has not been in use for many years.

Nilen: The second clue is in the twelfth photo, which shows the motorman's seat covered in blood.

Damien: This clearly indicates that the motorman was likely shot, possibly during a hijacking or due to other circumstances.

4. Second Phone ———————— Anil

The owner of the phone is Ankita Pulan, a 17-year-old who documented her experiences through a video.

She resided in Jaipur and attended Satyam College. Ankita traveled to Daman for her education and was in route to Jaipur to celebrate Christmas with her family.

She has a younger brother who is in the fourth grade. Ankita is active on social media platforms such as Facebook, Instagram, and YouTube.

She was born on October 27, 1970, and chose to study computer science with aspirations of becoming a computer engineer

Additionally, she carried some money for her parents and was traveling with friends that evening.

Upon examining her photo, I noticed a small bag said Alex. This bag was produced in 1884 in Telangana.

When I unzipped the first compartment, I discovered a small book belonging to Sandam Shan, a lawyer residing in Gandhi Nagar, Gujarat. He was born on May 15, 1959, making him approximately 28 years old at the time. The book also contained his phone number, but when I attempted to call, the phone was switched off.

It was noted that his sister had passed away at a young age.

The second compartment was empty, as were the third and fourth. However, upon further inspection,

I found a gold chain and a phone in a compartment resembling a bottle holder. A visit to a jewelry store revealed that the chain was valued at ₹120,000. The phone indicated that Sandam Shan was affluent, having owned a large house that was destroyed in a fire, prompting his relocation to Gandin Nagar.

He had previously lived in Silvassa but moved after the fire incident. Sandam had traveled to Daman to see friends and was planning a trip to Amritsar when one of his friends was involved in an accident.

Inside his phone, I found a diary entry dated December 16, 1987, in which he expressed his feelings to a dear friend, stating,

"I miss you. I will never forget what you did. I should not cross the road without looking from both sides.

I shouldn't have rushed to catch the train, it happened when we were going towards the railway station,

we were late for the train at night to Amritsar,

Suddenly there was an announcement 'train no. 04563 train to Amritsar will departure within a minute' so we ran without looking from both sides as we were going a truck suddenly came from nowhere towards them, it was at the very speed.

I didn't noticed but my friend noticed and shouted to stop but I was in a hurry so my friend came and pushed me to the end of the road

I was safe and sound but my friend met with an accident and died on the spot to save me.

How foolish of me I have his photo see this.

(seeing the photo)

I didn't knew that information can be this long isn't it said Theo, yes.

5. Wallet——————————Theo

As per me the wallet, this wallet is manufactured in 1986 I Comcoat company in Washington DC, United States of America.

When I opened it, I found a business card in which the name's owner is lee-choosing-col. He lived in south Korea and was later promoted and transferred to Washington DC. He had 2 meetings in India, first was in Daman, Gujrat and second was in Amritsar, Punjab.

When I checked the wallet, I found some Indian rupee, dollars and Korian won.

Then I found a driving license, passport, credit card of united states and a smart card.

When I opened the secret chain, I found a photo of his family, there were 4 members in his family.
See his photo
(seeing his photo)
When I rechecked the wallet I found a note, the note reads;
My dear son, I hope you are fine, I miss you. Keep this note always with you, for wherever you go I will always be there with you, no matter how hard the situation is, I will always be there with you.
From,
Your loving mom
To,
Lee-choosing-col
He was born in the year 1962. His mother died only 16 years old and his little brother who was just 10 years old was kidnapped.
Over the years he used to live with his father but due to Measles, his father died in 1983.

6. video——————————Nilen and Damien

Damien: According to the videos we could figure out that, we heard the scream of a women and a boy when we were at the platform and after that when we again heard that scream, the scream that we heard outside and inside were of the same women.

Is it a screaming contest that the same women! That same boy screams all day and night!

Nilen: similarly, when we heard the scream of the boy both inside and outside was of the same boy.
Damien: when we were searching for that sound, in this video we saw some food lying down at the very corner and when we were coming, we saw some suitcases lying behind the seats.
Nilen: but due to hurry we forgot to check what was in the suitcase but we zoomed and could only see the name tag.
Damien: That suitcase's owner's name is Aman Shing and he was from Amritsar.

Nilen: In addition to that, there was some bread, although it had been opened. Remarkably, despite the passage of years, it has not yet spoiled. This raises the question of how bread can remain unspoiled after being stored for such an extended period. Indeed, it is quite intriguing.

The science behind bread preservation often involves factors such as moisture content, the presence of preservatives, and the environment in which it is stored.

Perhaps this bread was made with some unique ingredients or stored in a way that inhibited mold growth.

It’s a curious anomaly that invites further investigation.

7. Newspaper ——————— Max

The newspaper appeared to offer no significant clues at first glance. The publication date was 13 December 1987, a seemingly ordinary day in history. However, upon examining page 5 more closely, I discovered a plea for help scrawled in a frantic hand.

The urgency of the message sent a chill down my spine. When I turned to the following page, the word 'help' was again inscribed, this time more desperate, as if the writer was reaching out in a moment of sheer panic.

On the subsequent page, I noticed blood—dark and ominous—staining the paper. Upon turning to that page, I found the haunting words.

'Mom, I miss you,' obscured by blood, a poignant reminder of loss and desperation. The juxtaposition of the mundane newspaper and the horrific messages within it created a stark contrast that was hard to ignore.

Damien: I suspect someone may have been murdered.

The evidence is compelling, and the emotional weight of those words cannot be overlooked. The blood, the pleas for help, and the mention of a mother all point to a tragic event that demands our attention.

Nilen: I share that suspicion. The implications of what we've found are disturbing. We need to dig deeper into the context of this newspaper and the events surrounding it.

Who was the author of those messages? What happened to them? The clues are there, hidden within the pages, waiting for us to uncover the truth.

8. 3rd phone ——————— Theo.

The owner of this mobile device is identified as Arand Dunam, a resident of Vadodara, Gujarat.
Arand recently embarked on a journey with his family, traveling from their home in Vadodara to the coastal town of Daman, and then onward to the historic city of Amritsar in Punjab.

The primary purpose of their visit to Daman was to spend time with his brother, who resides there.
Arand, a professional pilot, was born in 1961, and his career has taken him to various places, allowing him to experience the world from a unique vantage point.

Arand's educational journey began at Florida College in Texas, United States, where he pursued his passion for aviation. He achieved his dream of becoming a pilot at the young age of 22, a milestone that marked the beginning of a fulfilling career in the skies.

His mobile device holds more than just communication tools; it contains a diary that offers a glimpse into his personal life and thoughts.
Within its pages, Arand reflects on his relationships, including the six close friends he cherished.

Tragically, two of these friends lost their lives in a plane crash in Brazil during one of their adventures, a loss that undoubtedly left a profound impact on him. Family is of utmost importance to Arand.

He has two brothers, loving parents, and a grandmother who played a pivotal role in shaping his values and beliefs. His affection for his grandmother is particularly poignant; he often expressed that his love for her surpassed even his own life, highlighting the deep bond they shared.
This connection to his grandmother also fueled his creativity, as she inspired him to become an accomplished writer.
Arand has penned numerous poems, books, and Books, drawing from the rich tapestry of experiences and teachings she imparted to him.
The mobile device itself

is a remarkable piece of technology, manufactured in 1886, and it came with a hefty price tag of one lakh, indicating that Arand enjoys a comfortable financial status. This device not only serves as a means of communication but also as a repository of his thoughts, memories, and creative works. However, life has not been without its challenges for Arand and his family.

They faced a health crisis when the measles virus swept through their household, affecting each member.

Fortunately, they all managed to recover, but the ordeal took a tragic turn when one of his brothers succumbed to the illness after several months of struggle, passing away on April 14, 1983. This loss undoubtedly left a lasting mark on Arand.

9. Diary ——————— Celia

I was unable to ascertain the contents of the diary as it was secured with a robust lock.

Despite my efforts, I could not break it. The lock seemed to mock my curiosity, a barrier between me and the secrets that lay within its pages.

As I examined the diary closely, I noticed a brief inscription in the colophon. Upon further inspection, I discerned the time 12:30 AM, accompanied by a sequence of numbers: 28122017.

These figures appeared to shimmer, almost as if they were alive, pulsating with a hidden significance.

What on the earth would it glimmer?

What could they signify? I was at a loss, my mind racing with possibilities. "It might represent some sort of count, similar to the numbers we see when purchasing a book, which indicates the total number produced to date," suggested Anika, her brow furrowed in thought.

"Yes, that seems plausible," agreed Max, his eyes narrowing as he considered the implications of such a count.

The idea of a limited edition or a special release added an air of mystery to the diary, making it all the more intriguing. "Alternatively, the sequence 28122017 could denote the date 28 December 2017,

" Proposed Nilen, his voice steady and thoughtful.

"Indeed," was the consensus, but the date alone did not provide the clarity we sought. What had happened on that day?

Was it a significant event in Celia's life, or perhaps a turning point that led her to document her thoughts in this locked diary?

As we stood there, contemplating the possibilities, I felt a sense of urgency.

The diary was not just a collection of pages;

It was a vessel of memories, emotions, and perhaps even secrets that could change everything we thought we knew about Celia.

The shimmering numbers seemed to beckon us, urging us to uncover their meaning.

"What if we could find out what happened on that date?" I suggested, my mind racing with ideas.

"Maybe there are records or news articles that could shed light on it.

" We nodded in agreement, the spark of curiosity igniting a collective determination.

We decided to split up and gather information.

Anika would search online for any significant events that occurred on December 28, 2017,

while Max would head to the local library to sift through newspapers from that time.

Nilen, with his knack for research, volunteered to dig into social media archives.

Hoping to find any posts or mentions that could provide context.

But there was no trace of the date related to the train.

Wait! Wait! Interrupted Damien, could it be that tomorrow, 28 September 2017 is the date by which the train will arrive?

Yeah, I think it can be, so let's go to the railway station tomorrow on the train.

To investigate and to find the key to the diary's lock.

So, we will meet with our belongings at the railway station.
We will leave at 11:00 pm and reach there by midnight 12:15 am.

7

At railway station

The afternoon light had shifted to a muted silver, the sun hidden behind a bank of slow-moving clouds. The train's windows reflected the pale sky, making it harder to see outside, so that the world beyond appeared ghostly—trees smudged into green-grey shapes, fields fading into the horizon as though they were memories rather than places.

The air in the carriage felt still, as though it had been holding its breath for hours. A faint vibration rose from beneath the floor, steady yet uneven, carrying through the soles of shoes and into the bones.

The narrow aisle stretched ahead, empty and silent, its patterned carpet worn thin in the center from countless footsteps. Overhead, the faint hum of the lights wavered now and then, as though the electricity itself was growing tired.

At the far end, a door stood closed, its frosted glass panel glowing faintly from the light beyond. The handle gleamed in the dimness, polished by years of use, but something about its stillness felt deliberate—like a locked gaze that refused to break.

Outside, the scenery blurred into dark patches of forest, the occasional flicker of a farmhouse roof, then back into endless stretches of wild land.

Each time the train entered a wooded section, the light inside shifted subtly, deepening the shadows and softening the edges of everything.

Somewhere in the walls, a soft metallic tap sounded—irregular, almost like footsteps on a distant floor. Then it stopped, leaving behind a heavier silence than before.

The carriage resumed its quiet rhythm, but the air seemed different now, charged with an awareness that hadn't been there a moment ago.

It was the kind of silence that made a person turn their head, certain that something had just moved behind them.

11:00 PM

"Is everyone present?" Anil inquired, glancing around the dimly lit room. The air was thick with anticipation and a hint of anxiety.

"Yes, we must hurry; otherwise, we will miss the train. Let us proceed," replied Celia, her voice steady despite the urgency of the situation.

(Traveling to the railway station)

We hurried through the quiet streets, their footsteps echoing against the pavement. The night was cool, and the stars twinkled above, oblivious to the urgency of their mission.

(After some time)

As they approached the station, the faint sound of a train whistle could be heard in the distance, sending a jolt of adrenaline through their veins.

(After arriving at the station)

"We need to move quickly; it is already 12:20 AM, and the train is scheduled to arrive in 10 minutes. We must reach the platform in 3 minutes, so let us enter," Anil urged, leading the way through the bustling crowd.

"Will anyone stop us when we board the train?" Nilen asked, his brow furrowed with concern.

"Who would stop us? No one pays attention to the commotion or the train.
If by chance someone does confront us, we can claim to be foreigners who heard a scream from within the train and came to investigate, or we can devise some other excuse.

We must find a way to board the train," Celia reassured him, her eyes scanning the platform for any signs of trouble.

A sudden rumble filled the air, and they froze, their hearts pounding.

(Suddenly, the sound of an approaching train)

They initially thought it was another train, but then, unexpectedly, the very same old train they had previously traveled on appeared, its headlights cutting through the darkness.

"Hurry, or we will miss it! Quickly, let us move!" Celia shouted, her voice cutting through the noise of the arrival of the train on the platform.

Let's hurry, quickly.

8

Discovering a clue- A key

Evening had begun to settle, and with it came a subtle change in the air—a cooler weight, as though the train were gliding into a different kind of night. The sky outside was streaked with deep purples and faint embers of gold, fading quickly with every passing mile.

The rails sang a steady metallic note beneath the carriage, their rhythm almost hypnotic in the dimming light.

The windows reflected more of the inside than the world beyond now, showing faint, ghostlike outlines of the seats, luggage racks, and the narrow aisle that ran between them.

Shadows had deepened in the corners, clinging stubbornly to the edges where the weak glow of the ceiling lights couldn't quite reach

. A single bulb near the center flickered now and again, its brief flashes making the space seem alive with shifting shapes.

From somewhere far down the train came the faint sound of a door opening and closing, the metallic click carrying clearly through the otherwise quiet air.

A soft draught followed, curling through the carriage, bringing with it the scent of cold night air and the faintest hint of smoke.

The overhead racks rattled gently as the train swayed, and for a moment, it sounded as though something small had rolled within them before settling again.

Outside, silhouettes of trees swept past like dark sentinels, their branches reaching toward the train as if to snatch it from its tracks.

In the fading light, the horizon seemed to melt into the earth, leaving only a narrow band of deepening sky.

The moment felt suspended—caught between the last light of day and the first full breath of night.

It was a space in which anything could happen, where the next sound, however small, would feel impossibly loud and impossibly close.

After searching for ten minutes on the train, Nilen exclaimed, "Wait! Look what I found—a key."

His voice cut through the low hum of the train, drawing the attention of his companions.

"What purpose does it serve?" someone asked, curiosity piqued. Nilen shrugged, a mix of excitement and uncertainty in his eyes.

"For now, keep it in your bag. We will discuss it with the others later. Let's continue looking for more clues on the train.

" The group nodded in agreement, their minds racing with possibilities.

They resumed their search, scouring the compartments and peering into every nook and cranny.

After a while of searching, Damien inquired, "Did you find anything?" Celia shook her head, her brow furrowed in concentration.

"No, we didn't. What about you?" she asked, her voice tinged with hope.

"Yes, we discovered a key," Nilen interjected, "but we need to find the corresponding lock. Let's search for it together.

" The group rallied; their spirits lifted by the prospect of uncovering a mystery.

As they combed through the train, they examined every lock they could find.

After some time spent looking for the lock, they concluded, "We have examined every lock on the train—from the door locks to those on suitcases and even the small locks on children's toys, but none fit the key.

" Frustration began to seep into their voices.

"We have searched everywhere. I believe the key is useless; let's discard it," Anil suggested, his tone dismissive.

"I concur," Alex agreed, crossing his arms in resignation.

"Wait! Could the key possibly fit the diary we found earlier?" Anika proposed, her eyes lighting up with a spark of inspiration.

"Yes, that should be checked," Nilen responded, his enthusiasm rckindlcd.

"Theo, could you hand me that diary?" Nilen asked, his heart racing with anticipation.

"Of course, here it is," Theo replied, passing the worn leather book to Nilen with a sense of urgency.

With trembling hands, Nilen examined the lock on the diary, inserting the key carefully. To their astonishment,

It clicked open with a satisfying sound. "Quickly, open the diary and see what it contains," he urged, his voice barely above a whisper.

At 3:45 AM, they opened the diary and discovered a series of events listed with specific dates. The pages were filled with neat handwriting.

At that moment, the clock read 3:57 AM, its relentless ticking echoing in the otherwise silent compartment.

A sudden chill enveloped the space, creeping into my bones and leading me to believe that the train's temperature had been set to an uncomfortably low level.

The air felt thick and biting as if it had been pulled straight from the depths of winter, and I couldn't shake the feeling that something was amiss. How could it have become so frigid so quickly?

As the countdown approached the three-minute mark, an unsettling tension filled the air, amplifying the discomfort that had settled over us.

It felt as though we were confined within a cold storage facility, the kind where perishable goods are kept in a state of suspended animation.

The metallic hum of the train's machinery seemed to grow louder, a stark contrast to the eerie stillness that surrounded us.

We found ourselves trembling from the intense cold, our breaths visible in the air, forming small clouds that dissipated almost immediately.

I glanced around at my fellow passengers, their faces pale and drawn, eyes wide with confusion and concern.

Some huddled together, seeking warmth in shared body heat, while others wrapped their arms tightly around themselves as if that simple gesture could ward off the encroaching chill.

The overhead lights flickered momentarily, casting long shadows that danced across the walls, adding to the sense of unease that permeated the compartment.

With each passing second, the countdown loomed larger, a reminder of the impending unknown. What awaited us at the end of those three minutes?

The train rattled slightly as if responding to the tension in the air, and I could feel my heart racing in sync with the ticking clock.

The cold was no longer just a physical sensation; it had seeped into my mind, igniting a primal fear that something was wrong.

I shifted in my seat, trying to find a more comfortable position, but the chill seemed to seep through the fabric of my clothing, wrapping around me like a vice.

I could hear the soft murmurs of my fellow passengers, their voices barely above a whisper, sharing theories and speculations about the sudden drop in temperature.

Some suggested it was a malfunction, while others feared it was a sign of something more sinister.

As the seconds ticked away, I felt a sense of urgency building within me. I needed to know what was happening, to understand why we were trapped in this icy cocoon.

The countdown reached two minutes, and we could feel the chill air here.

So cold it was, that we were been frozen alive.It seemed like we were in Antarctica with no food and no shelter, only snow and ice. This situation arose during this movement.

9

Seeing the ghost on the train

Night had fully claimed the world outside, wrapping the train in a darkness so complete that the windows no longer showed scenery—only the faint, distorted reflections of the carriage interior.

The hum of the wheels had deepened into a low, steady growl, a constant reminder of the unseen miles passing beneath them. Somewhere in the distance, a mournful whistle echoed, stretching out into the emptiness before fading into silence.

Inside, the light was soft but insufficient, pooling weakly around the ceiling lamps and leaving the aisle in shifting half-shadows.

The motion of the train made those shadows sway and bend along the walls, as if something unseen were pacing just outside the reach of vision. The air was cooler now, touched by the faint scent of damp steel and night wind slipping in through the thin seams of the windows.

Every so often, the carriage trembled slightly, the metal joints groaning as though the train were resisting its own path. The sound carried through the floor like a muted heartbeat, irregular enough t

o be unsettling. Far ahead, a door creaked open, its hinges complaining before it closed with a solid, echoing thud that lingered far too long in the stillness.

Outside, brief flashes of light appeared—isolated signals or distant lamps—each one gone before it could fully register. They left ghostly afterimages in the eyes, like glimpses of a world that didn't quite match this one. The sky was a void, starless and heavy, pressing against the glass.

It was the kind of night that swallowed landmarks and blurred time, where hours could slip by unnoticed—or stretch endlessly.

Here, inside this small moving space, the only certainty was the sound of the rails and the unshakable sense that something unseen was moving with them.

Now only 1.5 minutes were left when suddenly the lights turned off like previously but were not dark,

we could see some blue light coming in our eyes, our eyes were shutting down because of such cold after some seconds we saw ice dropping down.

We could see a human's feet was covered with white smoke and also the surface of the train, we could only see feet because our eyes was shutting down infarct our eyes were shut because of the severe cold in our surrounding.

We couldn't see but Nilen and Damien hardly saw the face, the face was of a woman but pretended couldn't see.

After some seconds

As the train reached the station the coldness was gone and the temperature was normal and there was no ice,

what had happened, forget about it, let's hurry and get out of here.

At that moment, Nilen recalled that his phone had been left on the train.

I too had forgotten my phone on that train; therefore,

I will accompany Damien to retrieve both my phone and his camera before returning.

When they were entering the train, suddenly the train started, but luckily, just when they stepped on the train.

10

Separation of Nilen and Damien from others

The night had settled into a thick, almost tangible stillness, broken only by the train's steady rumble. The air inside the carriage felt heavier now, as if the weight of the miles behind and ahead pressed down upon it.

A faint vibration rose from the rails, climbing through the floor and into the bones, creating a sense of movement that felt more like drifting than traveling.

The lamps overhead glowed faintly amber, their light softened by dust-coated glass. It gave the carriage a muted warmth, though the corners remained steeped in shadow.

The aisle stretched ahead in a dim tunnel, each seat casting long, crooked shapes that shifted with the train's sway.

Every few moments, the faint metallic rattle of the windows punctuated the hum of the engine, like a subtle reminder of the thin barrier between inside and out.

Beyond the glass, the world was an unbroken darkness, occasionally fractured by the swift, silent passing of a solitary light—too far away to identify, too brief to make sense of. Each one felt like a fleeting signal, a message from somewhere deep in the night.

Somewhere toward the rear of the train, a sound stirred—a slow, deliberate creak, as though someone were shifting their weight on an old wooden step. It came once, then again, and then fell into silence, leaving the air heavier than before.

The atmosphere was thick with the sensation of being watched—not by a person, but by the night itself.

It pressed against the glass, clinging to the moving train as if unwilling to let it pass unnoticed. Inside, time seemed uncertain, marked not by minutes, but by the steady rhythm of the wheels and the unshakable feeling that each turn of the track was carrying them somewhere they had not meant to go.

After some time, we found ourselves confined within the train, the rhythmic clatter of the wheels on the tracks echoing our growing unease.

The dim lighting cast long shadows across the narrow aisles, and the air was thick with a sense of foreboding.

"Let us quickly retrieve the phone and the camera," I suggested, hoping that capturing some evidence of our surroundings might provide clarity or at least a distraction from our mounting anxiety. As time passed, Damien, unable to contain his restlessness, expressed his frustration, stating, "What should we do?

I am growing weary of sitting." His voice was tinged with impatience, a reflection of the claustrophobic atmosphere that enveloped us.

To which Nilen replied, "I share your sentiment. Let us search for some evidence related to this train." The idea of uncovering something—anything—that could explain our predicament sparked a flicker of hope.

Damien agreed, "Indeed, that is a sound idea. Let us proceed."

With a renewed sense of purpose, we began to explore the confines of the train. However, as we moved through the narrow corridors, a sense of uncertainty arose.

"Where should we look for them now?" one of us pondered aloud, glancing around at the seemingly endless rows of empty seats and closed compartments.

"I believe we ought to return to our investigation room," suggested another, recalling the small space where we had first gathered our thoughts. "That seems like a prudent plan.

Let us go," I affirmed, eager to regroup and strategize.

While aboard the train, Nilen inquired, "Did you discover anything here?" His voice was low, almost a whisper as if he feared disturbing the silence that surrounded us. "No, what about you?" came the response, equally subdued.

"Nothing as well," I admitted, a sense of disappointment washing over me.

At that moment, we overheard voices approaching, their laughter and chatter echoing ominously through the train.

As they drew nearer, our fear intensified, and we exchanged anxious glances, the weight of our situation pressing down on us like the heavy air in the compartment.

We instinctively moved closer together, our hearts racing as we strained to listen.

The voices were unfamiliar, and the tone was casual, almost mocking, as if they were unaware of the tension that gripped us.

"What if they find us?" I whispered, my mind racing with possibilities.

"We need to hide," Damien urged, his eyes darting

We were really frightened.

11

Teaming up with others.

The first light of morning had not yet touched the horizon, and the train moved through a landscape still trapped in night. The world beyond the windows was shapeless, only hinted at by the faintest gradations of grey against deeper black.

The glass itself was cool to the touch, slick with a fine film of condensation that blurred even those vague outlines.

Inside, the lamps burned low, as though reluctant to disturb the stillness. Their weak glow caught on the edges of the seats and the gleam of the luggage racks above, leaving the rest of the carriage in a hushed half-darkness.

Every movement of the train caused a slow ripple through the hanging straps, a lazy swaying that felt almost alive.

From somewhere along the roof came a soft patter—steady but irregular. It might have been rain, or perhaps the scattering of small debris shaken loose by the wind.

Now and then, the train would shift on its tracks, the low groan of metal stretching into the quiet like the sigh of some great sleeping creature.

The aisle was empty, yet the silence carried weight, as though footsteps had only just ceased. Faint sounds travelled easily here: the whisper of fabric brushing against a seat, the gentle clink of glass in a distant compartment, the nearly imperceptible hiss of air through a vent.

Far ahead, the faint outline of a door could be seen at the end of the carriage, its small window dark, revealing nothing of what lay beyond.

It seemed further away than it should have been, as if the space itself had stretched overnight. The train pressed on, steady but slow, carrying its passengers into a dawn that felt no closer than when the night began.

At that moment, someone opened the door, prompting us to scream in surprise.

However, we quickly realized they were not ghosts, but rather fellow humans.

"What brings you here?" we inquired. They explained, "We were merely traveling.

On December 29, 2007, we heard a scream, which led us to this location.

We are from 2007, but people here claim it is now 2017, so we decided to investigate."

"Coincidentally, we are here for the same reason and also intend to look into this matter," we responded.

"Would you mind if we collaborated on this investigation?" they asked.

"Of course, it would make the process easier for all of us," we agreed.

"Let us introduce ourselves," one of them suggested.

"My name is Nilen," said one. "I am Damien," added another.

"I am Dilen," followed by Peter, Emily, Dacy, Harry, and Caleb, each introducing themselves in turn.

We proceeded to share all the clues we had gathered and provided information about those who were not present with us.

After a while, one of us said, "I should call them to update them on our situation."

"I cannot make the call; my phone's battery is low," Damien replied. "Mine is too," Nilen added.

"Use my phone," Peter offered. "Thank you."

After a brief wait, Peter's phone began to ring, but the connection seemed unstable. Just then, the call connected.

"Hello, who is this?" Alex asked. "Hi, I am Damien," he replied, explaining the events of their journey and how they had come to meet.

"That's much better; we can now work together to resolve this issue. Stay safe and keep us updated about the diary. We will talk later. Thank you," Dacy concluded.

"Now, regarding that diary, when will the train make a stop?" she inquired.

"It is scheduled to stop at 6:00 AM," came the response. "What time is it now?"

"It is currently 5:50 AM." In approximately ten minutes, the train will stop, so let us be prepared.

12

The train reaches the platform

The first signs of dawn crept in reluctantly, painting the horizon in faint strokes of pale silver and muted rose. The train moved through the fragile stillness of that in-between hour when the night hasn't fully left, and the day hasn't yet taken hold. Outside, the land lay in soft shadows, its shapes vague and indistinct under the thin veil of early light.

Fields stretched endlessly on either side, their dewdrops catching the faint glimmer of the awakening sky.

Inside, the air was cool, touched with the faint, earthy scent of morning. The lamps above still glowed dimly, their light now competing with the growing brightness outside. It created a strange duality—half the carriage bathed in natural grey light, the other half still wrapped in the warm, artificial glow.

The effect was disorienting, as though the train existed in two times at once.

The rhythmic clatter of the wheels seemed gentler now, more measured, as if the train itself were moving cautiously into the day. A few distant creaks ran along the carriage frame, followed by the faint rattle of a loose panel overhead. Every sound carried in the quiet, amplified by the emptiness of the space.

Through the window, isolated shapes emerged from the haze—an abandoned shed leaning against the wind, a solitary telegraph pole standing like a sentinel, its wires trembling faintly. Occasionally, a shadow moved quickly across the land, only to vanish before its form could be understood.

The moment felt suspended, a fragile pause before the train's next turn. Though the light was growing, the air still held the hush of night, and with it, the strange sense that the world was holding something back—waiting, just out of sight, for the right moment to reveal itself.

After a duration of ten minutes, Emily announced, "The train is about to arrive at the platform.

" At that moment, the train came to a halt, and we swiftly disembarked.

While coming Dilen's bag oblivion fell and scattered.

Due to the darkness, he quickly kept his belongings un

Upon exiting, we were startled by a loud noise emanating from the train's main engine.

Curiously, we re-entered the train, only to find it empty.

What was perplexing was that we could hear the loud sound, yet the other passengers seemed oblivious to it.

Peter inquired, "What is the date?" To which the diary responded, "It is January 2, 1998.

" Peter expressed his astonishment, "How can it already be January 2, 1998? It was just December; how did January arrive so soon?"

"Let us investigate this matter tomorrow," suggested Dilen.

"Where should we go now?" Harry proposed, "Shall we find a comfortable hotel to stay in?"

"Yes, that sounds like a good plan. Let us proceed," came the agreement.

At the hotel, Damien suggested, "Let us rest for the night.

We can begin our investigation after breakfast tomorrow, if that is acceptable."

"Yes, please be ready by 9:00 AM," was the response.

(Morning, 9:00 AM)

"Let us commence our investigation," Dacy stated.

"Today is January 3, 1998," Peter confirmed. "But what is happening?

One moment it is 1998, then it shifts to 2017, and then to 2007.

What is the significance of these three years?" Nilen questioned.

"We will uncover the truth later, once we gather more clues or information," Harry replied.

Dilen asked, "What does the diary reveal? Is there any information regarding the train?"

Caleb pondered, "What is the connection between the train, December, and January?"

"We will resolve that later," was the consensus.

Meanwhile, during their discussion, Dilen exclaimed in shock, "What!

The next train is scheduled to arrive on December 7, 1998."

"That indicates an 11-month gap.

They must remain here for 11 months in 2017, while we are stuck in 1998," he concluded.

That night, while Damien was organizing his belongings.

He stumbled upon a cardholder belonging to an unknown individual.

He contemplated, "Should I inform them about this, now or wait until our investigation tomorrow?"

Yeah, I should wait until the investigation meeting starts. I should keep it safe until I show this clue to them.

13

Discovering a clue- Cards

The morning had strengthened, but the light that poured through the windows was pale and cold, carrying none of the warmth usually promised by daybreak. Outside, the landscape rolled by in muted tones—fields faded to ash-grey, distant hills softened by a fine mist that clung stubbornly to the earth.

Trees stood in sparse clusters, their bare branches swaying gently, tracing thin, dark lines against the washed-out sky.

The train moved steadily, its wheels striking the rails with a hollow, metallic rhythm that felt sharper in the stillness. Every joint and hinge in the carriage seemed to voice its age, creaking softly with each subtle shift in motion.

The air inside was cool, carrying the faint scent of damp wood and the lingering trace of smoke from somewhere far down the train.

Sunlight, where it managed to break through the cloud cover, fell in narrow strips across the aisle, gliding slowly as the train swayed. Dust motes drifted in those beams, turning lazily, their movement slow enough to make time feel stretched.

The luggage racks above sat mostly empty, their metal bars reflecting thin slivers of light, while the seats lay in an ordered, quiet row that made the space feel both calm and unnervingly still.

Through the window, a lone figure appeared in the distance—standing beside the tracks, unmoving, face indistinct in the mist. The image was there for only a breath before the train swept past, leaving only the impression of its presence lingering in the mind.

The sound of the rails deepened again, a low groan as the train curved gently into another stretch of countryside. The quiet that followed was not the peaceful kind; it carried with it a strange tension, as though something was traveling alongside them, keeping perfect pace just beyond the edge of sight.

4 January 1998

The atmosphere in the room was charged with anticipation as the group prepared to delve into their investigation. Dacy, with a determined look, initiated the discussion, "Has anyone uncovered any leads or information that could help us?"

Damien, who had been quietly reflecting on the events of their journey, finally spoke up. "Actually, I managed to gather some details while we were on the train. My bag slipped from the seat, and in the chaos of the flickering lights, I noticed something unusual." His voice was steady, but the urgency in his tone was palpable.

Emily, eager to take charge of the investigation, suggested a structured approach. "We have four cards in this card keeper. I propose we split into two groups to investigate each card systematically. This way, we can cover more ground and ensure we don't miss any crucial details."

The group nodded in agreement, and Emily continued, outlining the plan. "Here are the groups:

- The first card is the credit card. Dacy and I will take responsibility for gathering information regarding this card.

- The second card is the identity card. Nilen and Damien, you will investigate this card.

- The third card is the office card. Dilen and Harry will collect information about this card.

- The fourth card is the driver's license. Caleb and Peter, you will gather information on this card."

Dilen, always the organizer, added, "Let's make sure we reconvene to discuss our findings.

We have five days to collect the necessary information, so let's use our time wisely."

As the meeting wrapped up, Nilen suggested, "After an hour, we will have dinner, so let us return to our rooms and start our investigations."

9 January 1998

The day had finally arrived for the group to share their findings.

The atmosphere was a mix of excitement and nervousness as everyone gathered in the designated meeting room.

Dilen, taking the lead, addressed the group, "Is everyone prepared to present their findings? Let us begin with the credit card.

Emily and Dacy, please come forward to share the information you have gathered regarding this card."

Emily stepped forward, her notes in hand, while Dacy stood beside her, ready to contribute.

Let's start.

Expanded Narrative

1. Credit Card – Dacy and Emily

In the dimly lit room, Dacy and Emily sat across from each other, poring over the details of a credit card that had come into their possession. The card belonged to Arun Amir Pudhan, a name that echoed with a sense of familiarity.

Details of the Credit Card:

- Name: Arun Amir Pudhan
- Bank Name: Indian Bank
- Credit Card Number: XXXX XXXX XXXX XXXX (details redacted for security)
- Expiry Date: January 2000
- CVC Code: XXX (details redacted for security)

Emily had been the one to provide the specifics regarding the credit card. As they examined the card, it became evident that it had suffered extensive damage, rendering it unusable. The edges were frayed, and the magnetic strip was barely intact, suggesting it had seen better days.

"That concludes our findings," Dacy remarked, her voice steady but tinged with a hint of concern.

"Next, we will examine the identity card," Emily replied, her brow furrowing as she prepared to delve into the next piece of evidence.

2. Identity Card – Nilen and Damien

The identity card presented a clearer picture of Arun Amir Pudhan's life. Nilen and Damien scrutinized the information, piecing together the fragments of a man whose story was shrouded in mystery.

Details of the Identity Card:

- Name: Arun Amir Pudhan
- Date of Birth: December 19, 1975
- Residential Address: Karwan, Telangana
- Occupation: Designer
- Phone Number: 2134566XX (details redacted for privacy)
- House Name: Suman

"That is all the information available from the card," Nilen stated, his voice echoing in the silence of the room.

"We attempted to make contact, but the call did not connect," Damien added, his expression thoughtful.

In a bid to gather more information, Damien decided to reach out to a friend who lived in the same locality as Arun.

During his visits from the United States, he had often crossed paths with this friend, so he provided him with the house address listed on the identity card.

After a short while, Nilen's friend got back to him with some unsettling news.

The house had been unoccupied for a decade, as he was currently in 2008.

We found out,

Within the community and discovered that there were four individuals residing in that household. This household, once vibrant and full of life, had become a focal point of concern and curiosity for those around them.

The four individuals—each with their own unique stories and struggles—had formed a close-knit unit, supporting one another through thick and thin. However, their lives took a sudden and tragic turn one fateful day.

On that day, the owner of the cards, a man known for his meticulous nature and dedication to his work, had a crucial meeting scheduled. This meeting was of utmost importance, as it could potentially change the course of his career.

With a sense of urgency, he prepared for an unexpected trip from Daman to Amritsar, hoping to make a lasting impression on his colleagues and superiors.

He packed his belongings hastily, unaware that this journey would lead to unforeseen consequences. As night fell, the family gathered in their modest home, filled with a mix of anticipation and anxiety. They exchanged worried glances, knowing how vital this meeting was for their loved one.

However, as the hours passed, a sense of unease began to settle over them. The train, which was supposed to connect them to their hopes and dreams, had lost its connection somewhere along the way.

Communication lines were down, and no one seemed to have any information about its whereabouts. Tragically, that night became the most sorrowful for the family. News began to circulate that the train may have been involved in an accident, leaving the community in shock and disbelief.

The thought of their beloved family member being in danger was unbearable. As the reality of the situation sank in, the family was overcome with grief, their hearts heavy with worry and despair. In the wake of this tragedy, the family made the heart-wrenching decision to leave their home.

They felt an overwhelming need to escape the pain that had enveloped them, to seek solace in the unknown. With tear-streaked faces and heavy hearts, they packed their belongings, leaving behind the memories of happier times.

Their current whereabouts became a mystery, as they departed in silence, each member lost in their own thoughts and fears.

Efforts to prevent their departure were unsuccessful. Friends and neighbors, who had witnessed the family's struggles, tried to reach out, to offer comfort and support, but their pleas fell on deaf ears.

The family, consumed by their sorrow, felt that leaving was the only way to cope with the unbearable weight of their loss.

So, his family shifted to another country abroad to forget the sorrowful past that they had suffered through but couldn't.

3. Office card————————— Dilen and Harry

investigator Involved: Dilen and Harry

Name: Arun Amir Pudhan

Office Name: Designer Elementary Department

Office Address: Karwan, Hyderabad

Branches: The company operates in multiple locations, including Telangana, Daman, Chandigarh, Mumbai, Amritsar, Kochi, Chennai, Delhi, Lucknow, Srinagar, and Kolkata, as stated by Dilen.

Employment History:

This is Arun's second job. His first position was in a similar field, but he found it unsatisfactory due to an inadequate salary that did not meet his family's financial needs.

As a result, he sought a salary increase and ultimately decided to leave that role.

Arun began his first job at the age of 20 and departed after one year, at the age of 21.

He started his current position at 21 and continues to work here, as noted by Harry.

Driving License Details

Individuals Involved: Caleb and Peter

Name: Arun Amir Pudhan

Age: 22

Vehicle Types: Bike and Car

Card Number: 28377XXXXXXX

State of Issuance: Hyderabad

Valid Until: 15 September 2015

Blood Group: AB+

Additional Information:

That concludes the details regarding the driving license, as mentioned by Peter.

Upon contacting the driving department, we learned that Arun attended driving training with a friend. He faced challenges during his car lessons, failing three times before finally passing on his fourth attempt.

"Was that information necessary?" Emily inquired.

"That is all," Caleb responded.

"I believe we will uncover additional information when we visit Hyderabad and investigate further based on our respective cards," Damien suggested.

"When should we plan our visit?" Emily asked.

Dacy proposed, "How about 15 January 1998?" The group agreed, stating it was a good idea.

Travel Arrangements:

"I will arrange the flight tickets for us," Peter offered. However, Nilen raised a concern about finances. "Do not worry about the money; I can cover our expenses," he assured the group.

Final Preparations:

Thus, we have a perfect six days ahead. "Please pack your belongings, as we will be departing on the 15th, so be prepared," the group concluded, excited for their upcoming journey.

14

Going to Hyderabad

The clouds had thickened overhead, casting the world outside in a flat, shadowless light. The train slid through the countryside with a muted hum, its windows catching the dull reflection of the sky. Beyond the glass, fields stretched wide and empty, their edges blurred by a thin, restless mist that swirled in the wake of the wind. Every now and then, a dark shape—a crooked fence post, a leaning tree—emerged briefly from the haze before vanishing again into the grey.

Inside, the air was cool and still, touched by the faint tang of metal and old varnish. The ceiling lamps flickered faintly in rhythm with the train's motion, giving the aisle a strange pulse of light and shadow. The seats stood in perfect order, their fabric worn smooth, and in the far corner of the carriage, a single strap on the luggage rack swayed with the movement of the train, tapping softly against the metal frame.

A faint vibration rose from beneath the floor, steady but layered with occasional uneven beats—tiny shifts that made the silence feel more alive. Somewhere down the carriage, a hinge creaked, followed by the slow, deliberate sound of something settling into place.

Through the windows, the occasional railway sign flashed past—its letters unreadable in the blur—reminding anyone watching that the train was moving deeper into unfamiliar ground. The world outside had no landmarks now, only the endless stretch of pale earth and shifting mist.

It was a landscape without time, without change, as if the train were sliding through a moment that refused to end. Inside, the sense grew quietly but steadily that each mile carried them not toward a destination, but further into a place where the rules of the ordinary world no longer applied.

15 January 1998

The sun was just beginning to rise, casting a warm glow over the bustling city as Caleb glanced at his watch, anxiety creeping into his voice.

"Have you contacted the others in 2017?" he inquired; his brow furrowed with concern.

"Yes, I've informed them that we are departing for Hyderabad now," Damien replied, his tone steady but urgent.

"We need to hurry; we're already running late. If we don't arrive on time, we'll miss our flight.

Let's get to the airport quickly," Caleb urged, his heart racing as he imagined the chaos of missing their flight.

On the way to the airport

As they navigated through the morning traffic, Dilen turned to Caleb, his voice laced with curiosity. "When is our flight?"

"Our flight is scheduled for 8:00 am, and it's already 6:45 am.

We need to be at the airport by 8:15," Caleb responded, glancing nervously at the cars around them, hoping they would make it in time.

At the airport

They rushed through the airport doors, relief washing over them as they approached the check-in counter. "We made it on time. Now, please take your boarding passes as it's time for check-in," Damien announced, handing out the passes with a sense of accomplishment.

After the check-in

"Let's head inside quickly; the gate will close soon," Emily urged, her eyes darting towards the security line, which seemed to stretch endlessly.

After arriving in Hyderabad

Once they landed in Hyderabad, the excitement was palpable. "I’ve planned our itinerary. First, we should go to Hills Hotel," Emily suggested, her enthusiasm infectious.

At the hotel

As they settled into their rooms, Emily added, "Let’s take a moment to rest; it’s already 8:00."

"We’ll have dinner at 9:00 pm," Dacy mentioned, glancing at the clock and noting the time.

At dinner

The group gathered around a large table, the atmosphere buzzing with anticipation. "When should we begin the investigation?" Harry asked, his eyes gleaming with determination.

"We can start tomorrow; does that work for everyone?" Dilen replied, looking around the table for nods of agreement.

"Yes, that's fine," came the consensus, a wave of relief washing over them as they settled into their plans.

15

Investigation in Hyderabad

The mist outside had thickened into a low, rolling blanket, curling around the train as if trying to pull it from the tracks. Through the windows, there was little to see but shifting veils of grey that occasionally parted to reveal a hint of the landscape—a skeletal tree, a stretch of dark water, the glint of rails vanishing into the fog.

The effect was disorienting, making it difficult to tell if the train was truly moving forward or simply suspended in place.

Inside, the air felt denser, the quiet heavier. The usual sounds of travel—the metallic rhythm of wheels, the gentle sway of the carriage—seemed dampened, as though the mist outside had seeped in and absorbed them.

The lamps glowed weakly, their light swallowed by the shadows pooling in the corners. Every so often, a flicker in the far end of the carriage would draw the eye, but when looked at directly, it was nothing more than the shift of light over worn metal.

The aisle stretched empty and narrow, lined with seats that seemed to lean inward ever so slightly, their faded upholstery catching faint patterns of reflected light.

Above, the luggage racks stood mostly bare, but one strap hung loose, swaying with each subtle movement of the train—its soft tapping marking time in a way the muted wheels no longer seemed to.

A sudden shape swept past the window—a figure, perhaps, or simply the curve of a tree swallowed by the fog. It left no sound, no trace, only a tightening in the chest and a prickle along the skin.

The train pressed on, carving through the grey silence, each passing moment stretching longer than the last, as though time itself were caught in the mist, unwilling to let them go.

11:00 AM

The taxi has arrived.

Let's hurry, get in.

The excitement was palpable as the group quickly gathered their belongings and piled into the taxi. The driver greeted them with a nod, and they were off, the city blurring past as they headed towards their destination.

1:30 PM

We have arrived in Karwan; now we can explore various locations, and we will reconvene at Noble Park in Karwan, Emily suggested.

The group stepped out of the taxi, stretching their legs after the ride. The sun was shining brightly, and the air was filled with the sounds of the bustling city. Dilen pulled out his phone to check the time.

If you're running late, please give us a call, Dilen added.

Harry looked around, taking in the vibrant atmosphere. Let's head in our separate directions and regroup at 6:00 PM; we have a solid six hours to look into this issue, Harry stated.

With a nod of agreement, the group split up, each person eager to uncover the secrets of Karwan.

Let's go.

6:00 PM

Has everyone made it back? Yes, let's return to our hotel, Caleb said.

As the sun began to set, the group reconvened at Noble Park, each person buzzing with stories and discoveries from their day. I've already arranged for a cab, and it should be here shortly; oh, there it is, Damien remarked, pointing to the approaching vehicle.

On the way

Did everyone gather the necessary information? Peter asked, his curiosity piqued.

Yes, we did.

Shall we head back to Amritsar now that we have the details? Dilen inquired, glancing at the others for their thoughts.

Yes, he's correct; let's proceed to Amritsar, Dacy agreed, her enthusiasm evident.

Should I book the tickets for tomorrow's flight to Amritsar? Damien asked, pulling out his phone.

Yes, please do.

So, be ready; we will depart from Hyderabad to Amritsar at 7:00 PM tomorrow. be prepared by 5:00 PM, as we will leave for the airport at 5:15 PM.

Now, let's head to the Hills Hotel in Hyderabad.

Tomorrow, we will check out at 5:00 PM, so pack

your bags and have everything

5:00 PM

"Has everyone arrived?" Harry asked, glancing around the bustling room. "Let's head to the airport, but where is the cab?" His voice was tinged with urgency. "I booked it, and it just got here. We need to hurry; we must reach the airport on time, or we risk missing our flight." He checked his watch anxiously. "We should arrive by 6:00 PM."

At the airport

As they rushed through the terminal, Damien let out a sigh of relief. "We made it just in time," he said, glancing at the departure board. "Now, please take your boarding passes and proceed to check in quickly." The group hurried to the check-in counter, their hearts racing as they navigated through the throngs of travelers.

On the airplane

Once settled into their seats, Nilen turned to his companions, his curiosity piqued. "When will we arrive in Amritsar?" he asked, peering out the window at the clouds below. "We will get there tomorrow morning at 5:00 AM," came the reply from one of the flight attendants, who was making her rounds. The hum of the engines filled the cabin as the plane ascended into the sky, and the group settled in for the journey ahead.

In Amritsar

5:00 AM

As the plane touched down, the early morning sun began to rise, casting a golden hue over the city. "Let's head to the hotel and share our story," Harry suggested, excitement bubbling in his voice. The group gathered their belongings and made their way through the airport, eager to start their adventure.

6:30 AM

Arriving at the hotel, they quickly checked in and dropped off their bags. "Now, let's refresh ourselves and take a short nap," Damien proposed, stifling a yawn. "We will begin the investigation meeting at 11:00 AM." The promise of rest was welcomed, and one by one, they retreated to their rooms, ready to recharge for the important tasks that lay ahead.

Let’s start the investigation.

Beginning with the first card is the credit card by Emily and Dacy.

Credit card ——————————— Emily

And Dacy

Upon our arrival at the Bank of India (BOI), we were struck by the establishment's antiquated appearance.

The faded paint on the walls and the worn-out furniture gave the impression that time had stood still within its confines.

As we stepped inside, the atmosphere felt unusually quiet, with only a handful of patrons scattered throughout the spacious lobby, each seemingly lost in their own thoughts or transactions.

We made our way to the counter to check the balance on a card that, the card was expired which had an amount of RS 20,000.

The cardholder, who had intended to transfer these funds to an international credit card, was unfortunately caught up in pressing matters that required him to travel to Amritsar, as Dacy had informed us.

The urgency of his situation seemed to overshadow the financial transaction he had planned.

Weeks passed, and the bank manager, who was also the cardholder's cousin, made several attempts to reach out regarding the transfer plan. However, his efforts were met with silence; he was unable to establish contact with the cardholder. In a bid to gather more information, he reached out to the cardholder's family, only to find that they too were in the dark about his whereabouts. The situation grew increasingly concerning.

A month later, the bank manager received alarming news: the train that the cardholder had taken was reported missing.

This revelation sent shockwaves through the small community, yet, despite the gravity of the situation, no one—neither detectives nor authorities responsible for locating missing persons—seemed to take any initiative to investigate the matter.

The lack of action was disheartening, especially considering the personal connection the bank manager had to the cardholder.

Before he could fully articulate his concerns or thoughts on the troubling situation, we felt an instinctive urge to leave the bank.

Something about the atmosphere felt off, and our intuition urged us to exit.

As we made our way out, we were relieved to realize that we had managed to gather all the important information we needed, as Emily had pointed out.

Among the details we collected was the identity card belonging to Nilen and Damien, which added another layer of complexity to the unfolding narrative.

The entire experience left us with a sense of unease, as we pondered the implications of the cardholder's disappearance and the mysterious circumstances surrounding it.

The antiquated bank, once a mere stop on our journey, had transformed into a focal point of intrigue and concern, intertwining our lives with that of the missing cardholder in ways we had

Identity card————————————Nilen and Damien

Upon arriving at the office, we began inquiring with the other employees, but Dilen reported that they had no information.

We encountered a staff member who was familiar with thc cardholder.

He mentioned that the day before the train incident, the cardholder had asked him to arrange train tickets.

The cardholder often delegated tasks to this staff member, whom he trusted like a brother, allowing him to handle such responsibilities.

"That's all we discovered," Harry stated.

Nilen raised a question, wondering why they were seeking information about this individual.

Damien explained that the goal was to trace the train and gather details that could unravel the mystery, enabling them to return home sooner.

Emily added, "I believe Alex and others in 2017 must-have uncovered some details regarding the train."

Dilen emphasized the need to gather more information about the train within the next ten months.

Next, we turned our attention to the fourth card, the Driving License, with Caleb and Peter.

Driving License – Caleb and Peter

Upon our arrival, we spoke with the person in charge and obtained details about the cardholder's residence and the information listed on the identity card.

We also learned about a friend of his who frequently visited, and we requested and received his contact number.

It turned out that this friend had intended to accompany them but was unable to do so due to the sudden death of a relative in an accident.

16

Going for further investigation.

The fog outside had begun to thin in places, revealing fragments of a landscape that felt both near and impossibly far. Low, rolling hills emerged like islands from a grey sea, their slopes dotted with dark, leafless trees that stood motionless against the pale sky. The ground glistened faintly, as if coated with a thin layer of frost, catching the weak light that filtered through the clouds.

Inside, the train was hushed, the air still holding the cool bite of early morning. The ceiling lamps hummed faintly, their glow uneven, making the aisle appear to waver in brightness. Shadows clung stubbornly to the corners, softening the outlines of seats and luggage racks until they seemed part of the gloom.

A faint scent of damp earth drifted in through a barely sealed window, mingling with the metallic tang of the rails.

The steady rhythm of the wheels was there, but something about it had shifted—its tempo slightly slower, its tone deeper. Now and then, a hollow clang echoed from somewhere far down the train, the sound carrying and fading like a bell tolling in the distance.

Through the window, shapes moved along the edge of the hills—perhaps animals, perhaps tricks of the light—but they never came close enough to see clearly.

The eye would catch them in the corner of vision, but by the time the gaze fixed on them, they had already vanished.

The feeling inside the carriage was not of danger exactly, but of crossing into a place where the rules were unfamiliar. The air seemed charged, like the moment before a storm breaks. And though the train rolled onward, the thought lingered that it might not be traveling through space alone, but through something else entirely.

We visited the residence of his friend, a place that held countless memories for both of us.

As we stepped inside, the atmosphere was thick with nostalgia, and it wasn't long before he became quite emotional.

He expressed, with a tremor in his voice, that his friend meant more to him than a brother.

This declaration resonated deeply with me, as I understood the weight of those words.

We had shared everything throughout our lives, having been inseparable since kindergarten.

Our bond was unparalleled; we played, studied, and celebrated festivals together, creating a tapestry of experiences that defined our childhood.

We spent countless afternoons engrossed in movies and cartoons, laughing until our sides hurt, and dreaming about the future.

Those moments were the foundation of our friendship, a sanctuary where we could be ourselves without fear of judgment. Yet, amidst the joy, I often felt a twinge of jealousy.

He consistently outperformed me academically, and his playful teasing about my grades stung, even if I never held it against him.

Deep down, I admired his brilliance and was proud to call him my closest friend.

Now, as I reflect on those days, I find myself longing for the sound of his laughter, a melody that once filled my life with joy.

I miss him dearly, and if he were here now, I would love to recount a story or two, sharing the laughter and camaraderie that defined our school days. Those memories are a bittersweet reminder of the fun and laughter we once shared, a stark contrast to the silence that now envelops my heart.

In my quest to locate him, I have faced nothing but frustration.

My efforts have been in vain, and the absence of his presence weighs heavily on me.

He confided in me, sharing his secrets and problems, believing I could help him find solutions. We were truly inseparable, two halves of a whole, navigating the complexities of life together.

But then, tragedy struck when I was just sixteen.

It was my birthday, a day that should have been filled with joy, but instead, it became a turning point in my life.

My parents were involved in a devastating accident, leaving me without a place to go, even among relatives who seemed to turn their backs on me in my time of need.

It was then that my friend's parents graciously invited me to stay with them, offering me refuge when I felt utterly lost.

That moment is etched in my memory forever, a beacon of kindness in a dark time, and recalling it brings tears

After a week of anxious waiting, we received the shocking news that the train my friend was on had gone missing.

It was a chilling revelation that sent waves of fear and uncertainty through all of us who knew him. What was particularly alarming was the absence of any detectives or law enforcement officials actively investigating the situation.

It felt surreal that a train could simply vanish without a trace, and the lack of urgency from authorities only deepened our sense of dread.

When his family learned of the incident, they were utterly devastated.

The weight of the unknown was unbearable, and the thought of their loved one potentially being in danger was too much to bear.

In their grief and desperation, they made the difficult decision to leave their home behind, seeking solace and perhaps a fresh start in Bhopal, a city in Madhya Pradesh known for its rich history and vibrant culture.

The move was not just a physical relocation; it was an emotional escape from the haunting memories of what had transpired.

At that time, I had my income, which provided me with a sense of stability amidst the chaos.

With a heavy heart but a determined spirit, I decided to purchase a house just outside the city. It was a modest dwelling, but it represented a new beginning, a place where I could support my friend's family during this tumultuous time.

I envisioned it as a sanctuary, a space where they could find comfort and healing as they navigated the uncertainty of their situation.

The house became a symbol of hope, a reminder that even in the darkest of times, there is the possibility of light and new beginnings.

In his remembrance, I wrote a poem.

Alden Dalmet

I am not a good writer.

The poem starts now said Caleb speaking from his friend.

My dear friend

I still cherish the memories we shared,

Playing together, enjoying every moment.

When I felt alone,

With nowhere to go,

You opened your home to me,

Offering shelter and solace.

We faced challenges together,

Finding solution side by side,

But however, on that fateful day

Everything changed.

I searched for you endlessly,

But found no trace,

Eventually, I had to accept,

Yet, my heart still echoes with joy and pain.

Every time I think of you,

Tears well up in my eyes,

Though I go through my days,

Your memory never fades away.

With tears that blend joy and sorrow,

If I've ever hurt you, I apologize,

Feel our friendship deep within,

It's a bond that's truly artful.

I thank you for all you've done.

You planted hope where none had grown,

You erased all my past misdeeds,

With your kindness and your good deeds.

You're more than a brother to me,

Alden Dalmet

I wish I could repay you,
You'll always remain my friend,
For poets like us are destined.

A good friend is more than family,
For they stand by you faithfully,
In times of need, they're a beacon,
Truly life's greatest salvation.

As I reminisce about us,
I write this poem,
With you, my friend,
In solitude.

When the news arrived,
Your family departed,
Sadness still lingers,
Echoing through the house.

What happened to you,

To our friendship too,

We once held truth and courage,

Where did it all go.

As the sun sets on this poem,

with a poignant conclusion,

I vow never to forget you,

For we are still the best of friends.

Just then, time was up, and he had to leave for a meeting out of town.

He mentioned that if you come across any information, please let him know.

Then we departed. That's all we could uncover, Peter stated.

Now let's pause the investigation for today. We need to rest, said Emily.

17

Going to Tamil Nadu

The sky had darkened again, though it was not yet evening. Heavy clouds had gathered low, their edges bruised with shades of deep violet and steel. A fine drizzle streaked the windows, turning the outside world into a shifting watercolor—shapes dissolving and reforming with each sway of the train. The fields beyond were sodden, their grass bending under the weight of rain, while thin streams of water traced erratic paths through the soil.

Inside, the carriage carried the faint scent of damp wool and metal, as though the wetness outside had seeped in through the seams. The lamps overhead glowed a little brighter against the gloom, but their light pooled only in small circles, leaving much of the space in a soft, shadowed haze.

The faint patter of rain on the roof blended with the hum of the wheels, creating a muted rhythm that felt almost hypnotic.

Every so often, the train would cross a stretch of uneven track, and the resulting jolt would send a tremor through the entire carriage. Luggage straps swayed in response, and somewhere overhead, a panel gave a brief metallic creak before settling again.

Outside, shapes flickered by—bare trees standing close to the tracks, their branches so near they seemed to scrape against the train's side. In the distance, the faint glow of a small settlement appeared—a cluster of lights, warm against the cold landscape—but it vanished almost as soon as it was seen, swallowed by the curve of the tracks and the tightening mist.

The sense here was not of motion toward something, but of slipping deeper into a place both unfamiliar and watchful. The rain softened the world, but it also blurred the boundaries, making it harder to tell where the journey was leading—or if it was meant to end at all.

20 January 1994

I received the update that we would soon have details regarding the train.

The anticipation hung in the air like a thick fog, and I could feel the excitement bubbling within me.

So, who will accompany me? I mean, does everyone want to join me in Tamil Nadu? asked Damien, his eyes sparkling with enthusiasm.

"Yes!" everyone replied affirmatively, their voices overlapping in a chorus of eagerness.

The prospect of traveling together filled us with a sense of camaraderie and adventure.

"Shall I go ahead and book tickets for 23rd January 1998?" Damien inquired, already pulling out his phone to check for availability.

"Absolutely, that sounds good," came the enthusiastic response from the group.

"First Hyderabad, and now Tamil Nadu," Damien continued, his mind racing with the possibilities of the journey ahead.

“I have a thought lingering in my mind; I must have been there when I was younger,” Dilen remarked, a hint of nostalgia creeping into his voice.

“Will I be able to see myself again?” Dilen pondered aloud, his expression turning contemplative.

“Well, that remains a mystery,” Dacy responded, her tone light yet thoughtful.

“We used to live in Tamil Nadu, but after the bomb blast, my family decided to leave that house and move to Amritsar,” Dilen shared, his voice tinged with a mix of sadness and reflection.

“We believed life would be challenging there, so we considered it too risky.

Thus, we vacated the house,” he continued, the memories flooding back.

“However, I cannot recall the exact date of the incident since I was quite young and unable to determine my age,” Dilen explained, his brow furrowing as he tried to piece together the fragments of his past.

“So, pack your bags and belongings because we are heading to Tamil Nadu tomorrow,” Damien announced, his voice firm and decisive.

“But we were planning to leave in 2 to 3 days,” Nilen interjected, a hint of confusion in his tone.

“Yes, but I can't wait that long; there are no available flights during those days, and tomorrow is the last flight for a week,”

Damien stated, urgency creeping into his voice.

“Our flight departs at 7:30 PM, and we need to arrive by 6:30 PM,” he added, glancing at his watch as if to emphasize the ticking clock.

“Let’s have dinner first, and then we can pack our bags”.

21 January 1998

3:00 PM

We will be departing in approximately three and a half hours.

Is there anything anyone would like to ask? Damien inquired; everyone responded with a no.

6:30 PM

We need to hurry; the taxi has arrived.

At the airport

7:00 PM

You are aware of the procedure, so please take your boarding passes, and let's proceed swiftly.

18

Airplane's air turbulence

The rain had eased, but its presence lingered in the slick sheen of the rails and the soft, rhythmic drip from the carriage roof. Outside, the world was washed clean yet somehow muted, the colors drained into shades of grey and dull green.

Low clouds hung close to the earth, their bellies heavy and slow-moving, casting a dim, even light that erased shadows from the land.

The train's motion was steady but quieter now, as if it were treading carefully over the wet tracks. The sound of the wheels had taken on a softer, rolling hum, broken only by the occasional metallic clink from beneath the floor.

Through the windows, narrow dirt paths wound away from the rails, disappearing into distant groves of trees that looked darker and denser than the rest of the landscape.

Inside, the air was cooler, touched by a faint draft that slipped through the thin cracks of the window frames. The smell of damp earth was stronger here, mixing with the faint, lingering scent of oil and aged wood.

The light from the lamps seemed more subdued than before, their glow dulled by the moisture in the air, as though even the bulbs themselves were weighed down by the weather.

The aisle was empty, and the silence within the carriage felt layered—quiet, but not hollow. Every faint sound seemed to carry meaning: the creak of a hinge far down the train, the soft thud of something settling in the next compartment, the slow sway of a strap overhead tapping gently against the metal rack.

Through the misted glass, a dark shape appeared briefly at the edge of a field, unmoving and indistinct. Before the eye could make sense of it, the train passed, leaving behind only the unsettling thought that it might still be there, watching.

In the aircraft, the atmosphere was initially calm and filled with the hum of conversation as passengers settled into their seats, ready for the journey ahead.

For the first hour, everything proceeded smoothly; the flight attendants moved gracefully down the aisles, offering refreshments and ensuring that everyone was comfortable.

The plane soared through the skies, the sun shining brightly, and the view from the windows was nothing short of breathtaking.

However, this tranquility was abruptly shattered when, without warning, the plane lost its signal system.

Just as the heavy downpour began, the skies darkened ominously, creating unfavorable flying conditions that sent a ripple of unease through the cabin.

The pilot's voice crackled over the intercom, breaking the tense silence.

He informed us that landing was not an option, as we had already passed all over India and were now flying over the vast expanse of the Indian Ocean. The realization that we were far from any land heightened our anxiety, especially since our fuel levels were dwindling after a brief stop in Bangalore before heading to Tamil Nadu.

The weight of the situation pressed down on us, and the cabin, once filled with chatter, fell into a hushed stillness.

As the turbulence intensified, some passengers began to pray fervently, their voices rising above the roar of the storm outside.

Others were in tears, their faces pale with fear, while many were visibly shaken, gripping their armrests tightly.

The atmosphere was thick with tension, and the uncertainty of our fate loomed large.

As we approached the Maldives, the pilot's voice returned, this time tinged with urgency. He informed us that our fuel reserves were critically low, with only ten minutes of fuel left.

Panic surged through the cabin as we realized the gravity of our situation.

Five minutes later, the oxygen masks deployed with a sudden hiss, and the aircraft began a gradual descent.

We instinctively donned the masks, the cool plastic a stark contrast to the rising heat of anxiety.

The pilot's voice was steady as he announced the necessity of a water landing, instructing us to put on life jackets while sending a distress signal to the control tower in hopes of receiving assistance.

The reality of our predicament settled in, and the gravity of the moment was palpable.

Suddenly, through the rain-smeared windows, we spotted a beam of light cutting through the darkness, illuminating a large landmass that could potentially be the British Indian Ocean Territory. With no other alternatives and time running out, the pilot made the critical decision to attempt a landing on this land.

As we descended toward the ground, the aircraft began to shake and jolt violently, a clear indication that we were encountering turbulence.

The sudden and unexpected turbulence sent a wave of anxiety through the cabin, but the flight crew remained calm and focused.

Despite the unsettling conditions and the knowledge that the plane's landing system had sustained damage during the flight, the pilots made the critical decision to proceed with the landing.

With the roar of the engines and the sound of the wind rushing past, we braced ourselves for a challenging touchdown.

The aircraft swayed and dipped as it approached the runway, and the tension in the cabin was palpable.

Passengers exchanged worried glances, some clutching their armrests tightly, while others whispered prayers or reassurances to one another. Finally, with a jarring thud, the wheels made contact with the tarmac.

The landing was far from smooth; the plane skidded and veered slightly, but the pilots skillfully regained control, guiding us to a safe stop.

The relief that washed over us was immense, but it was tinged with the stark reality of what had just transpired.

In the aftermath of the landing, we learned that out of the 85 passengers on board, three had tragically lost their lives, and 52 others had sustained various injuries, some serious.

The news was devastating, a somber reminder of the fragility of life and the unpredictability of air travel.

Yet, amidst the chaos and fear, we found ourselves among the fortunate ones.

We emerged from the ordeal relatively unscathed, both physically and emotionally, our belongings intact and our spirits shaken but resilient.

As we disembarked, the gravity of the situation settled in.

We were survivors of a perilous landing that could have ended in disaster. The experience bonded us in a way that words could hardly capture, as we shared knowing looks and silent acknowledgments of the harrowing journey we had just endured.

We were required to remain in the British Indian Ocean Territory for a total of 21 days, as the date was 22 January 1998.

This extended stay was necessitated by the complete absence of any information regarding our plane, which was the subject of an ongoing investigation.

The situation was particularly distressing, as we were left in a state of uncertainty and anxiety, unsure of when we might receive news or be able to return home.

During this time, it was determined that we were indeed located in the British Indian Ocean Territory, a remote and isolated area that added to our feelings of vulnerability.

To seek assistance and clarity, we made several attempts to contact the relevant authorities. However, our efforts were thwarted by a powerful cyclone that struck the region on 25 January 1998. This natural disaster severely disrupted all communication signals, leaving us cut off from the outside world and further complicating our situation.

The cyclone persisted for five long days, during which time flights were prohibited due to the dangerous weather conditions.

The howling winds and torrential rain made it impossible for any aircraft to operate safely, and we were left to contend with the elements.

As the storm raged outside, we had no choice but to take shelter in a hotel, which became our temporary refuge amidst the chaos

The hotel, while providing some comfort, was filled with other stranded travelers, all of us sharing the same sense of uncertainty and concern for our safety.

19

Arrival at Tamil Nadu

The light outside had thinned to a dull, metallic grey, the kind that seemed to drain the color from everything it touched. The landscape had grown emptier—long stretches of open ground broken only by the occasional tangle of wild grass or the skeletal remains of a fence leaning into the wind. The rails ahead shimmered faintly, slick with leftover rain, stretching into the distance until they vanished into a low bank of fog.

The train moved at a steady, measured pace, the sound of the wheels echoing in a deeper register now, almost like a slow, distant drum. Each turn of the track brought the faint groan of the carriages, the wood and metal shifting in their age-old conversation.

Inside, the lamps gave off a warm but narrow glow, leaving the far corners of the carriage in shadow. The air smelled faintly of damp cloth and machine oil, a mix that seemed sharper with each mile. The faint draft along the aisle carried a chill that slid unnoticed at first, then lingered on the skin.

Through the windows, occasional shapes appeared—clusters of stones, a rusted signal post, the black outline of a lone tree standing far from any others. Once, the train passed a narrow bridge spanning a trickle of dark water; the view was gone almost before it had formed, replaced again by the shifting grey of the open land.

Somewhere toward the rear, there was the faint, irregular sound of something moving—a slow scrape, then silence, then the almost imperceptible creak of weight settling. It came from no particular place, yet it felt close.

The steady motion of the train continued, but it carried with it an unspoken truth: whatever lay ahead was no more certain than what lingered unseen behind.

We returned to Tamil Nadu on February 11, 1998, at 8:30 PM. Upon our arrival, Dilen expressed his excitement, stating,

"I have finally returned to my hometown after so many years.

" We decided to stay at a hotel for the night, planning to visit Dilen's childhood home the following day.

At the airport, we encountered a minor issue when security questioned why the year on our documents was listed as 2007.

We clarified that it was simply a printing error.

On the evening of February 11, 1998, during dinner, I outlined our plans for the next day:

- 8:00 AM: Breakfast

- 8:30 AM: Check out

- 8:45 AM: Depart for Dilen's town

- 10:00 AM: Arrival

- 10:15 AM: Hotel booking

- 10:30 AM: Investigation time

- 11:00 AM: Visit Dilen's house

"That should suffice for now," Peter remarked.

On February 12, 1998, at 8:00 AM, Nilen urged us to have breakfast quickly before checking out.

By 8:30 AM, Dacy confirmed that it was time to leave.

At 8:45 AM, we hailed a cab, and by 10:00 AM, we had finally arrived at our destination, where we anticipated finding answers to our questions.

Caleb noted, "We should have been there by now," to which Emily replied, "We're almost there; it's just about a mile away.

" After five minutes, Peter announced, "We've finally arrived.

" Dilen expressed his eagerness, saying, "I can see my house from here, and it looks well-maintained."

As we approached, Harry reminded Dilen, "You must have lived here when you were younger." Dilen then instructed the driver,

"Stop the cab! I'll get out here to avoid the traffic jam on this narrow road."

Caleb confirmed, "You remember that!" Dilen insisted, "I want to go alone;

it won't feel right otherwise." He added, "I'll start recording with my spy camera."

"I'm heading in now," Dilen said, "but please ensure you start recording as soon as I enter the house."

"Alright, I'll take care of it," came the response.

20

Reaching Dilen's house

The clouds above had deepened to a uniform slate, stretching endlessly in every direction. The air outside seemed heavier now, as though it pressed down on the land, flattening the fields into muted swathes of brown and grey. Every so often, the train passed through a shallow dip in the earth where water had gathered—wide, dark pools that mirrored the sky and trembled at the disturbance of the passing wheels.

The train's rhythm was steady, but slower, each turn of the axles sounding deliberate, almost cautious. The gentle rocking of the carriage created soft patterns of light and shadow across the aisle as the lamps swayed ever so slightly overhead. Their glow was warm but confined, unable to reach the furthest edges of the space, where shadows seemed to thicken rather than fade.

A faint draft slipped along the floor, carrying with it the scent of wet soil and something faintly metallic—like the lingering trace of rain against iron. The upholstery of the seats felt cooler than before, holding the chill of the day. Somewhere far down the corridor, a quiet click echoed, followed by the muffled sound of a latch catching. It was not loud, but it stood out sharply against the low hum of travel.

Through the windows, the scenery changed with deceptive slowness—occasional clusters of bare trees, a scattering of stones piled into rough cairns, the brief flash of a distant farmhouse roof before it disappeared again behind the curve of the land. Each landmark seemed isolated, cut off, as though it belonged to a different world entirely.

The sense inside was not of mere travel but of passage—through space, through time, and perhaps through something less tangible. The train pressed on, but the weight of the air suggested that whatever lay ahead was already aware of its approach.

As I approached my childhood home, the same beautiful place where I learned to eat, sing, laugh, talk, walk, and share both my joys and sorrows while confronting life's challenges, memories flooded back.

The familiar scent of the blooming lilacs in the front yard wrapped around me like a warm embrace, and the sound of the wind rustling through the trees seemed to whisper secrets of the past.

Upon entering, I vividly recalled a moment with my mother, who was trying to console me after I received poor grades on an exam, leaving me feeling downcast.

I could almost hear her gentle voice, soothing and encouraging, reminding me that failure was just a stepping stone to success.

As I stepped inside, I encountered my younger self, a small boy with wide, curious eyes and an innocent smile that mirrored my own.

My mother, bustling about in the kitchen, greeted him with a curious, "Hello, yes?"

Her voice was filled with warmth, and I could see the love radiating from her as she prepared dinner, completely unaware of the extraordinary moment unfolding before her.

Although my family did not recognize me, my younger self felt an inexplicable connection, as if a thread of familiarity wove between us.

He introduced himself as my friend who had come to visit, a clever ruse that seemed to satisfy my mother's curiosity.

"But you didn't mention your friend," she said, her brow furrowing slightly in confusion.

My younger self, with a sheepish grin, replied, "I forgot to tell you.

" There was a innocence in his voice that tugged at my heartstrings, reminding me of the carefree days of childhood.

Afterward, he led me to my room, a space filled with books and the remnants of countless adventures.

The walls were adorned with drawings I had created, each one a snapshot of my imagination.

As we sat on the edge of the bed, he looked at me with a mix of wonder and suspicion.

"Who are you, and why do you seem so familiar?" he asked, tilting his head slightly as if trying to piece together a puzzle.

"I am Dilen, but I am you from the future," I explained, my voice steady despite the surreal nature of the moment.

"I traveled here by train." The words felt strange on my tongue, yet they held a truth that resonated deep within me.

"But how can this be possible?" my younger self questioned, his brow furrowing in confusion, the gears of his young mind turning rapidly.

But how is this possible, said my younger self.

Yeah, I know.

I can’t believe this, are you lying?

No! why would I lie?

Ok, ok if you don’t believe me, I have one way.

21

Dilen's saying comes true

The afternoon had grown unnaturally dim, the sun hidden behind a wall of low, unbroken cloud. The world outside passed in hushed, muted tones—stretches of pale grass, clusters of thin, leafless trees, and occasional flashes of dark, wet stone jutting out from the earth.

The horizon was close, blurred by a fine haze that seemed to move with the train, keeping pace no matter how far it traveled.

The wheels sang a steady metallic rhythm beneath the floor, their tone slightly hollow, as though the rails were suspended over empty space. Inside, the lamps burned faintly, their yellow light pooling onto the worn carpet in uneven shapes. Shadows crept into the corners of the carriage, shifting gently with the sway of the train, giving the impression of movement where none should have been.

A soft vibration ran through the walls, followed by the faintest sound—like the brush of cloth against metal. It came and went, without pattern, too deliberate to be the wind, too subtle to be machinery.

The air was cooler here, edged with the faint scent of damp wood and steel.

Beyond the window, a weathered signal post flashed past, its paint flaked and peeling, its purpose unclear. Farther along, a lone figure stood at the edge of a distant embankment, its shape still and unblinking. The sight was gone in an instant, leaving only the memory of it—and the quiet unease it stirred.

The train pressed forward, yet the view outside barely changed, as if it were circling within the same stretch of land over and over. Inside, the silence between each creak, each sigh of the carriage seemed to grow longer, heavier, as though the train itself were listening for something it expected, but had not yet heard.

What is the current time and date? It is 12 February 1998 at 10:46 AM.

This afternoon, an incident will occur involving your best friend Helon, and you will witness it firsthand. Is that so? Indeed, let us observe.

I am not the sole individual who has traveled from the future; my companions accompanied me during that period.

However, please keep this information confidential; this discussion must remain between us and my friends.

Please bring your friend along; I will join you at approximately 4:00 PM.

Inform your friend about this, but refrain from mentioning that an accident will take place at the crispy waffles shop.

A truck will arrive, and while you will be unharmed, your friend will not survive.

Now, I must take my leave; we will reconvene at 4:00 PM with your friend.

As time was running out, I departed in a cab and relayed all the details.

That afternoon, at 4:00 PM, I arrived at my younger self's residence.

Upon entering, I encountered my friend who had perished in an accident many years ago.

I introduced myself and engaged in conversation.

My younger self claimed that I was his cousin who had come to visit.

As we proceeded toward the shop, I leaned in and whispered to my younger self that a robbery would occur there shortly before the accident.

No sooner had I spoken than a group of robbers stormed the shop and fled.

However, my younger self dismissed my warning, attributing it to mere coincidence.

As we approached the shop, I sensed that this was a critical location.

I noticed a vehicle approaching us.

I cautioned him that the vehicle appeared to have brake failure, but he remained skeptical.

Having lost my best friend in my youth, I am determined not to lose my younger self as well.

22

Dilen's sacrificing save

The light outside had dulled into a uniform grey, with no clear source, as though the sky itself had forgotten the sun. The landscape was flat and empty, a vast stretch of muted earth broken only by the occasional solitary tree, its branches reaching outward like black veins against the pale horizon. The air beyond the glass looked still, heavy, and untouched by wind.

Inside, the carriage felt almost sealed off from time. The lamps glowed with a tired warmth, their light catching the curve of the windows and the polished edges of the metal luggage racks above.

The aisle lay in quiet shadow, the carpet worn in the center by countless unseen travelers. Each sway of the train caused the loose strap on the rack to tap gently against its frame—a slow, rhythmic sound that was too steady to ignore.

The wheels beneath struck the rails in a low, rolling beat, though every so often, the rhythm stuttered for just a fraction of a second before finding its pace again. The brief interruptions seemed small, but they left behind an odd, lingering unease.

Outside, distant shapes sometimes appeared through the haze—stone posts in crooked rows, the glint of water lying still in shallow pools, the dark, sloping roof of an isolated structure that vanished almost before the mind could register it.

Each glimpse felt disconnected from the next, as though the train were passing through fragments of different places rather than a continuous stretch of land.

Somewhere far down the train, a metallic sound rang out—a sharp, hollow echo that carried down the corridor before fading into the hum of the wheels. It came only once, but it stayed in the mind, joining the growing sense that this journey was not simply forward—it was deeper.

The vehicle accelerated rapidly and was now merely three meters away when I made my appearance.

As it drew closer, I took a perilous risk and pushed both individuals out of harm's way.

They fell to the ground just as the vehicle grazed my hand, ensuring that we all emerged unscathed. Although my hand was fractured,

I felt a profound sense of relief for having saved my friend and my younger self.

Tears streamed down my face as I reflected on a painful memory from my past.

It was a time when I had been injured, and my friend had selflessly pushed me to safety, ultimately sacrificing his own life.

His bravery and friendship remain etched in my heart, and I continue to miss him dearly.

The vehicle collided with the shop, but I found solace in having protected my younger self and my friend,

even if I struggled to articulate that feeling. The sight of the driver, bloodied and panicked, surrounded by onlookers and the arrival of an ambulance, was harrowing.

Tragically, the driver succumbed to his injuries almost immediately due to the speed of the impact.

I glanced at my younger self and my friend, who were rendered speechless and eventually fainted. As the ambulance arrived, I too lost consciousness. When I regained awareness, I found myself surrounded by friends and noticed my fractured hand.

Everyone expressed their gratitude, particularly my parents and the parents of my friend, who thanked me for my actions.

That night, I was discharged from the hospital. Upon my release, my younger self approached me and said,

"I am sorry, and I thank you for saving me. I now fully believe in you."

This was merely the beginning; others were waiting for us.

I sensed that something significant would occur this week, though I could not predict what it would be, so we needed to remain vigilant.

I suggested that let's go out for lunch the following day.

My friends and I planned to meet at noon.

At 9:00 PM, while at the hotel, I heard, "What a save! Incredible, Dilen!" to which I replied, "Yes, I know."

9:30 PM

In Dilen's room,

(Dilen writing in a diary)

12 February 1998

Thursday

9:30 PM

Dear Diary,

As I sit here, pen in hand, I find it increasingly difficult to articulate the profound sorrow that has settled in my heart, stemming from a tragic event in my childhood—the death of my only best friend.

The weight of that loss has lingered with me through the years, a shadow that never quite fades.

I vividly recall the day he saved my life, a moment that is forever etched in my memory, a bittersweet reminder of both his bravery and the fragility of life.

Today, however, I had the opportunity to save a friend of mine, someone who may not recognize me, yet I hold a deep understanding of him.

This experience has evoked a complex blend of sadness and joy within me; I mourn the loss of my friend from so many years ago while simultaneously feeling a sense of fulfillment for having honored his sacrifice.

It's as if the universe conspired to give me a second chance, a way to repay the debt I owe to my fallen friend.

In my youth, I distinctly felt my friend's presence before that fateful incident, a warmth and camaraderie that filled my days with laughter and adventure.

We were inseparable, two halves of a whole, until that tragic moment when everything changed. His sacrifice remains etched in my memory, a haunting reminder of the fragility of life and the bonds we share.

The story began with a simple walk to the store, a mundane task that turned into a life-altering event. As I strolled along, lost in thought, a vehicle suddenly approached, its headlights blinding in the dusk.

Time seemed to slow as I realized the danger, but it was my friend who acted instinctively. He noticed the threat before I did, and in a split second, he pushed me out of harm's way, placing himself in the vehicle's path. Despite his desperate efforts to save himself, it was tragically too late; the vehicle collided with him, and the world around me shattered.

I witnessed the horrifying scene unfold before my eyes, my friend lying there, motionless and covered in blood. Panic surged through me as I rushed to his side, my heart pounding in my chest. He looked at me, his feelings, love, sacrifice; I still remember right now at this movement. “Don’t worry, I will call for an ambulance immediately,” I exclaimed, my voice trembling with fear, he quoted “It is my time to go, but be happy and remember me.” With those final words, he passed away before me, his blood flowing freely.

I wept, feeling utterly helpless. Now, it is my turn to honor him.

Before he died, I made a promise: “I will do something for you one day! I promise.” Today, I have fulfilled that promise. Thus, I conclude this entry in memory of you, Dilen.

——————The End——————————

I miss you, my friend.

I will never forget you.

Good night.

23

The dog's save.

The sky outside had deepened into a heavy, slate-grey dome, pressing low over the land. The air beyond the windows seemed thick, as if it held weight, muting the colors and flattening the world into shades of cold steel and ash. Occasional bursts of wind stirred the grass into brief, restless waves, but otherwise, the landscape remained still—too still.

The train's motion was steady, though slower than before. The wheels rolled over the tracks with a deep, resonant hum, the sound carrying through the floor and into the seats. The occasional metallic groan of the carriage frame added to the impression of an old machine working against an unseen strain.

Inside, the lamps offered their usual muted glow, yet the shadows they cast seemed darker, clinging stubbornly in the corners.

The aisle stretched narrow and empty, the patterned carpet showing faint scuffs where countless feet had once passed.

A faint draft curled along the floor, cold enough to sting the skin where it touched.

Through the windows, the scenery shifted in slow, deliberate frames: a cluster of leaning fence posts, a sagging bridge crossing a trickle of black water, the pale outline of a figure far in the distance.

Each sight appeared briefly before the train carried it away, leaving behind a sharper awareness of the emptiness in between.

Somewhere toward the middle of the carriage, a faint sound stirred—a single, deliberate click, like the turning of a latch. It came once and did not repeat, but its presence lingered, sharp in the silence.

The air seemed to tighten after it, as though the train itself had heard and was waiting for whatever came next. The journey pressed on, but with each mile, it felt less like travel and more like descent.

13 February 1998

The clock on the wall ticked ominously, reminding us that time was slipping away. We must hurry; it is already 11:30 AM.

The air was thick with anticipation as we gathered our belongings, ready to embark on our planned outing. He has arrived; let us proceed.

As we made our way to the door, we formed a circle, each of us taking turns introducing ourselves.

My younger self, with a hint of shyness, also shared his name, his voice barely above a whisper.

Now, let us continue.

With excitement bubbling in our hearts, we stepped outside into the crisp morning air.

On our way to the restaurant, however, our plans took an unexpected turn.

We encountered an abandoned dog.

It was a pitiful sight, its fur matted and eyes filled with a mixture of fear and hope.

We felt compelled to adopt him, to give him the love and care he so desperately needed.

This golden retriever was truly beautiful, despite his disheveled appearance.

His coat shimmered in the sunlight, and his gentle demeanor tugged at our heartstrings.

How could anyone abandon such a creature? Thus, we decided to take him in, to offer him a second chance at life.

As we approached a nearby bus stop, the dog suddenly began to bark, his voice sharp and urgent. We wondered what could be causing this commotion.

Uncertain of the reason, we initially ignored it, thinking perhaps he was simply excited. But the dog began to pull us along, his instincts guiding him.

We followed at a distance, curious yet cautious, as the dog led us to a large, bushy tree. There, he approached other individuals, barking insistently, as if trying to communicate something important.

Meanwhile, some people fled the bus stop, their faces etched with fear, raising our suspicions.

But we chose to disregard it, caught up in the dog's fervor.

The barking grew louder, more frantic, as if he sensed something we could not.

As we moved further away, an explosion erupted from the bus stop, a deafening roar that shattered the morning calm.

Fear and panic set in, our hearts racing as we instinctively ducked for cover.

While we were unharmed, the dog, our brave companion, sustained serious injuries in the chaos.

In the aftermath, the scene was one of devastation. Many lives were lost in the explosion.

The air thick with smoke and the acrid scent.

But because of that dog, we were here right now or dead.

We were not worried about us, we were worried about the dog, the life savior.

Due to the explosion, the dog was badly injured for calling the other who were around the bomb around the bus stop.

We were unable to call for an ambulance in time, so we quickly sought assistance from a nearby passerby.

Hoping they could help us reach the hospital as swiftly as possible.

The urgency of the situation weighed heavily on us as we rushed to the car, our hearts racing with worry for our beloved dog, Dilen.

Upon our arrival at the hospital, Emily immediately approached a doctor, her voice filled with desperation.

"Do you have accommodations for the dog? He is injured; we need help immediately," she pleaded, her eyes wide with concern.

The doctor, maintaining a calm demeanor despite the chaos, responded affirmatively.

"Yes, please take him to the operating room quickly. However, you all are not permitted to enter the operating room."

He instructed his tone firm yet compassionate. He then added.

"There is a possibility that the dog may not survive the thorough operation,

If that occurs, we cannot be held responsible.

Please sign here as acknowledgment.

" The weight of his words hung in the air, and one of us, trembling with anxiety, complied and signed the consent form.

Our hearts were heavy with the uncertainty of what lay ahead.

As the hours dragged on, each minute felt like an eternity.

I turned to my companions, trying to process the gravity of the situation.

"I cannot believe it; for the first time in my life, I witnessed a truly selfless and brave dog who has prioritized the safety of others, especially us," I remarked.

Reflecting on how Dilen had bravely shielded us from danger moments before the accident.

Just then, the operating room doors swung open, and the doctor emerged, a beaming smile breaking through the tension that had enveloped us.

"The operation was successful; the dog is now out of danger," he announced, his voice filled with relief.

"Only his tail and back right leg are injured, and the wounds will heal within 15 days."

A wave of relief washed over us, and we exchanged glances of gratitude and disbelief.

Dacy, still processing the news, noted, "This confirms that Dilen was right; something significant occurred today."

Her words resonated with us, a reminder of the bond we shared with our loyal companion and the extraordinary events that had unfolded.

At that moment, we felt a renewed sense of hope, knowing that Dilen would soon be on the road to recovery.

We would be there to support him every step of the way.

24

Investigation in haunted house

The land outside had taken on a strange sameness, as if the train were moving through a loop of repeating scenery. The same low, grey hills rose in the distance, the same clusters of skeletal trees leaned into the still air, and the same narrow strip of dirt paralleled the tracks before vanishing into nothing. Even the light seemed unchanged—dull, muted, without the rise or fall of a sun.

The wheels turned with a slow, deliberate rhythm, their sound low and hollow. Every so often, a faint metallic ping echoed from beneath the carriage, sharp against the otherwise even hum.

The movement of the train was steady, but the air inside seemed restless, as though holding a quiet current that brushed faintly against the skin.

The lamps burned in their usual dim glow, yet the space they lit seemed smaller now, the aisle narrower, the shadows closer.

The luggage racks stood empty, their metal rails glinting faintly in the light, while the seats sat in perfect, undisturbed rows. A faint scent of cold air and something faintly earthy lingered, seeping in through unseen cracks.

Outside, a lone signal post appeared, leaning at an angle, its faded markings unreadable as the train passed. Moments later, a stone wall emerged from the mist, running alongside the tracks for only a few seconds before ending abruptly, as if it had been cut away. Then came nothing—just the familiar emptiness once more.

Somewhere far ahead, a muffled thud sounded, distant yet distinct, as though something heavy had shifted. The sound was swallowed almost instantly by the hum of the rails, but its memory stayed. The train pressed forward, deeper into the repetition, leaving the unsettling question of whether it was truly moving forward at all.

Fifteen days had passed since the incident, and the inquiry regarding the dog's condition was finally made.

The atmosphere in the small clinic was tense with anticipation as the doctor entered the room, clipboard in hand.

"How is the dog feeling now?" he asked, his voice steady but laced with concern.

The owner, visibly relieved, responded, "Yes, he has made a full recovery; we can discharge him now." The doctor nodded, a smile breaking through his professional demeanor.

However, he quickly added, "I must emphasize the need for the dog to rest for an additional 12 to 13 days.

It's crucial for his complete recovery."

"We will ensure that he gets the necessary care," the owner assured him, gratitude evident in their voice.

With that, the doctor departed, leaving behind a sense of relief and hope.

As the owner gathered their belongings, a sudden notification chimed from a phone that had been resting quietly on the table.

It was a sound that had never been heard before, and it startled everyone in the room.

"Read the message," suggested Caleb, leaning closer to the device.

"It's not mine," Peter replied, furrowing his brow. "But we do not know who it belongs to, so perhaps you should check it," Nilen advised, his curiosity piqued.

"You are correct; let us read it," Harry added, his eyes glinting with intrigue.

"Let's wait until we reach the hotel to read it," one of them suggested, wanting to maintain the moment's privacy.

"Yes, that seems prudent," came the agreement, and they all nodded in unison, their minds already racing with possibilities.

Later that evening, at the hotel, they gathered around the dining table, the aroma of food wafting through the air.

Laughter and chatter filled the room, but the mystery of the message lingered in the back of their minds.

Finally, they decided it was time to unveil the secret. With a collective breath, they opened the message.

It was from someone named Kalish, and the content sent a chill down their spine.

The message warned of a haunted house adjacent to Rights Park, situated deep within the nearby forest.

"This message is programmed to auto-pop after three months," Peter noted, his voice low and serious.

"However, the phone was turned off for the past three months, so it did not receive any messages until now."

"Should we investigate this further?" Damien inquired; his eyes wide open.

Yes, sure; why not? I am not afraid of any ghosts, let the ghosts come towards me.

I will show them the way to the gates of hell, that stupid ghost, I can handle it with my little finger.

Don't worry, you all stay behind me.

Nothing will happen except that ghost whom I will beat hard till she says sorry, said Caleb confidently with his overconfidence.

Let's see, replied Max.

14 February 1998

7:30 PM Let us proceed.

As we ventured forth into the encroaching darkness, the atmosphere thickened around us. The shadowy forest loomed ahead, its gnarled branches reaching out like skeletal fingers against the overcast sky.

The air was alive with the sounds of insects buzzing, their incessant hum mingling with the low rumble of the car engine, creating a symphony of unease.

Each sound seemed amplified in the stillness, as if the very forest was holding its breath, waiting for our next move.

It felt as though we were moving toward a lion, a predator lurking in the shadows, its presence palpable as we attempted to evade its grasp.

The thrill of adventure was tinged with a sense of foreboding, a primal instinct urging us to turn back. Yet, the question lingered in our minds: was it truly a ghost that awaited us, or merely a fabrication of our overactive imaginations? As we passed a graveyard, a chill ran down my spine.

The sight of the dilapidated house adjacent to it sent a wave of trepidation through our group; an unsettling feeling enveloped us like a thick fog.

The house stood there, weathered and worn, its windows dark and hollow, as if it wcrc watching us. Could this be the haunted house we had been seeking, the very place where legends whispered of restless spirits?

To verify our suspicions, we consulted the internet on our phones, the glow of the screens illuminating our anxious faces.

The search confirmed our fears; the park had indeed transformed into a graveyard, a resting place for souls long departed.

Thus, it was confirmed that we had found the haunted house, the epicenter of our ghostly quest. As we approached, a black cat suddenly darted across our path, its sleek form disappearing into the underbrush.

Peter, ever the skeptic, remarked that if Ravi were present, he would caution us against proceeding, claiming that a black cat crossing our path was a bad omen.

He dismissed it as mere superstition, but the unease in the air was palpable. "Indeed, you are correct," Dacy replied, her voice barely above a whisper, as if acknowledging the weight of the moment.

As we drew closer to the house, Nilen voiced his concerns, his brow furrowed with worry. "Maybe we should turn back," he suggested, glancing nervously at the looming.

No need to move back, why are you afraid, nothing will happen with you, just be with me, said Caleb confidently.

As we stepped deeper into the haunted house, the air grew thick with an unsettling chill, and the flickering shadows danced ominously along the walls.

The piano's haunting melody echoed through the corridors, weaving a tapestry of eerie notes that seemed to beckon us further into the darkness. Each note resonated with an otherworldly quality, sending shivers down our spines, but Caleb, with his unwavering confidence, led the way, his eyes sparkling with excitement rather than fear.

Nilen and Damien, the first pair, moved cautiously to the right, their flashlights cutting through the gloom.

The beam of light revealed faded portraits hanging crookedly on the walls, their subjects appearing to watch us with hollow eyes. "Do you think they're watching us?" Nilen whispered, a hint of trepidation creeping into his voice.

Damien chuckled nervously, trying to lighten the mood. "Just old paintings. They can't hurt us." But even he couldn't shake the feeling that something was amiss.

Meanwhile, Dilen and Harry took the left path, where the air felt heavier, almost suffocating. As they walked, they stumbled upon a dusty old trunk, its lock rusted and barely hanging on. "What do you think is inside?" Dilen asked, his curiosity piqued. Harry, ever the skeptic, shrugged. "Probably just old clothes or junk. But let's check it out." They pried it open, revealing a collection of tattered letters and a faded diary.

But old and dusty.

Caleb and Peter pressed forward, their footsteps echoing in the silence.

Caleb's heart raced with anticipation.

"I can feel it, Peter.

We're getting closer to the source of that music." Peter nodded; his brow furrowed in concentration. They entered a grand room adorned with cobwebs and dust-covered furniture.

In the center stood an ornate piano, its keys moving as if played by invisible hands.

"This is it," Caleb breathed, his eyes wide with wonder.

"This is where the music is coming from."

Meanwhile, Emily and Dacy navigated the narrow path behind the stairs, their flashlights illuminating the way.

The walls were lined with strange symbols and markings that seemed to pulse with energy.

"What do you think this means?" Dacy asked, tracing her fingers over the carvings.

But Caleb wasn't, since childhood, he wasn't afraid of ghosts, vampires, etc.

He loved to watch, read, and hear horror and adventure.

As we explored the house, it was semi-darkness all around, some of us bought a torch with them, so they switch on the torch and began searching for clues.

We divided ourselves into 2 people.

1st group: Nilen and Damien in the right direction

2nd group: Dilen and Harry in the left direction

3rd group: Caleb and Peter in the front direction

4th group: Emily and Dacy in behind the stair's direction (small path in that direction)

After searching in our respective direction, we will together go upstairs, to find out, who is playing the piano.

When I make a call that means you should come to this place, said Peter

We went in our respective directions to find clues.

As Nilen and Damien were searching for clues, suddenly Nilen tripped off something, the thing was a book, just then there was a call,

That means they have called us, let's go,

So Nilen quickly kept it in his bag and followed Damien.

After reaching there,

Hey friends, did you get any clues? said Harry.

Yes, said Nilen

Suddenly, from somewhere upstairs there was a sound, so the conversation was left incomplete.

A sudden noise emanated from somewhere above, interrupting our conversation.

It was a sharp, jarring sound that sliced through the air, causing us all to pause mid-sentence.

As we exchanged nervous glances, the noise grew louder, echoing through the dimly lit hallway like a haunting melody.

It was as if an unseen orchestra was tuning up, each note rising in intensity, pulling us toward the staircase that spiraled upward into the unknown.

Leading the way was Caleb, the bravest among us, his determination evident in the set of his jaw and the way he gripped the banister.

The rest of us trailed behind, our hearts pounding in our chests, each step echoing our trepidation. Upon reaching the first floor, the highest level of the house, we were met with an eerie silence that contrasted sharply with the cacophony we had just experienced.

Two doors stood before us, each shrouded in mystery.

The first room was locked tight, with a heavy wooden door adorned with a sign that read "No Entry."

The warning felt like a finality, confirming that the sound could not possibly originate from there.

We exchanged glances, a silent agreement passing between us that we would not venture into the forbidden space.

The second room, however, beckoned us with an unsettling allure.

It was unguarded, devoid of any lock or notice, yet a red cloth was ominously wrapped around the door handle.

The fabric fluttered slightly, as if alive, and the inscription upon it sent chills down our spines: "Don't open or death."

The warning was stark and foreboding, yet it only fueled our curiosity.

"I'm telling you again, let's go back," urged Nilen, his voice trembling slightly.

He was the most cautious of our group, always the first to sense danger.

"There's no point in retreating; we're at the final stage, let's see this through," countered Caleb, his voice steady and unwavering.

"Caleb is right," Peter agreed, his eyes gleaming with excitement and fear.

The thrill of the unknown was intoxicating, and we found ourselves drawn to the door despite the warning.

As we approached the room, a palpable fear gripped us, tightening around our throats like a noose.

Yet, Caleb, emboldened by the adrenaline coursing through him, mustered the courage to remove the cloth.

With a swift motion, he pushed the door open.

We saw that the ghost was playing a piano and crying.

Her face was red, dressed like a funeral ware, and her hands pale white.

That was the movement we were shocked.

Peter mistakenly touched a flower vase and it broke.

The apparition became aware of our presence and turned to look back, and we were met with mutual astonishment.

Her face was ghostly pale, with eyes that glowed a deep red, resembling tears of blood. Her expression conveyed a mix of anger and hostility as if we were her adversaries from years past.

As her face flushed with rage, her breathing quickened, and her fists clenched tightly, filled with resentment.

Upon seeing us, she let out a piercing scream; in that instant, Nilen and Damien recognized her as the same figure they had encountered on the train.

With no choice but to escape the haunted house, we attempted to flee.

Everyone dashed away, except for Caleb, who stood frozen in fear.

Peter grasped his hand and pulled him along.

The ghost pursued us relentlessly, making it feel as though we were fleeing from a ravenous lion intent on our destruction, as Dilen remarked.

"Forget the lion; focus on that terrifying ghost chasing us," someone urged.

As we sprinted, the ghost shouted, “You have made a grave mistake by coming here.”

We ran as fast as we could, but she was gaining on us, nearly reaching Caleb.

Fortunately, a photograph of a young boy, around six or seven years old, diverted her attention.

The ghost let out a heart-wrenching cry, leaving us to wonder whose photograph it was.

If she hadn't stopped, we might have faced dire consequences.

Thankfully, she paused, tears streaming down her face, suggesting a deep connection to the boy in the picture.

But what were we supposed to do about it? Once we finally escaped the house.

We took a moment to breathe easily, relieved to be free from the ghost's grasp.

Caleb remained in shock, prompting Emily to suggest we take him to the hotel.

What happened Caleb? you were about to kill that ghost and show them the gates of heaven, oh sorry, hell right? Said Dilen

But Caleb couldn't answer because he was still traumatized.

At the hotel, we decided to let him rest while we had dinner.

After our meal, we noticed Caleb was asleep and agreed it was time for us to rest as well.

Damien proposed a meeting for our investigation the next day at 11:00 am, to which Nilen agreed.

“How’s the dog?” Nilen inquired. “He’s fine,”

With that, we wished each other goodnight.

25

Discovering a book

The world outside had narrowed to a ribbon of track surrounded by an endless sweep of muted grey. The horizon was barely distinguishable from the sky, the two blending into a single, unbroken expanse.

Every so often, the faint outline of a hill or a scattering of low bushes emerged, only to dissolve again into the haze before the mind could hold onto them. The effect was disorienting—like moving through a place that refused to be remembered.

The wheels beneath carried their steady rhythm, but there was a new undertone to the sound—a faint, almost imperceptible tremor, as if something in the mechanics strained against itself. Occasionally, a sharper metallic note rang out, echoing through the floor, before the hum returned to its familiar monotone.

Inside, the lamps glowed faintly, their light reduced to small, trembling pools along the aisle. The shadows seemed heavier now, pressing inward, making the carriage feel narrower than before.

A thin, cool draft slid along the floor, curling around the base of the seats and vanishing as quietly as it came.

Through the fogged windows, fleeting shapes appeared—low stone ruins scattered in a field, the twisted remains of a wooden post, the distant silhouette of something tall and thin standing against the sky.

Each was gone in moments, leaving behind an odd sense that they might reappear at any turn.

From somewhere toward the rear of the train came the faint sound of movement—slow, deliberate, and unhurried. It didn't match the rhythm of the wheels, didn't belong to the machinery. It paused, then continued, as though following its own path within the motion of the carriage.

The journey pressed on, but with each passing mile, the air inside grew thicker, as though the train was carrying not just its passengers, but something else entirely.

April 1, 1998

How are you feeling now? I am well, thank you for your assistance; let us commence the investigation meeting.

There is little to discuss, as only some paperwork remains, which I can handle.

Shall we take a few days to rest? Damien suggested. You are correct; let us take a break for a few days and reconvene on April 13, 1998.

April 13, 1998

Let us begin the meeting, Damien stated. Did anyone uncover any clues in that house? Dilen inquired. Yes, Nilen replied to Dilen

What did you find? Nilen responded, I nearly fell, but I discovered this book. Let us examine it.

The book contains the following entries:

1. January 6, 1997

2. May 3, 1997

3. June 17, 1997

4. November 27, 1997

5. December 1, 1997

6. December 7, 1997

7. December 8, 1997

Harry remarked, that this ink appears different, and the handwriting is distinct from the others, written in red ink.

But what did this mean hold? is it even a clue or just a random date? questioned Caleb.

Let us stop the investigation about this diary, it can't be called a clue, it is completely clueless, so let's stop discussing the clue rather than the train.

It can be worked as a clue but not a clue so, we will carry it with us in case of need, answered Max.

Hold on! Did anyone realize that she was the individual we saw on the train?

I believe our vision was impaired due to the intense cold. While it seems, our eyes were mostly closed, I (Nilen) and Damien could see somewhat, Nilen added.

We have not communicated with those from 2018, Caleb noted.

I used to call them daily, but I was unable to reach them, Damien mentioned.

Should we attempt to contact them? Nilen proposed.

(call connected)

In 2018, a year marked by significant events and personal journeys, a group of friends found themselves entangled in a mystery that would take them across the country.

"Greetings! Greetings!" Theo's voice echoed through the phone, filled with enthusiasm and curiosity.

"Indeed, Nilen," he continued, "how are you and how are the others?

Why did you not reach out, and what progress have you made regarding the clue?" His tone was a mix of concern and eagerness, reflecting the urgency of their quest.

"We are well, Nilen," replied Dilen, his voice slightly muffled as if he were still waking up.

We were unable to call because we were asleep, and you consistently contact us at 9:00 AM.

We must rise early to search for the clue, yet we have not been successful.

There was a hint of frustration in his words, a testament to the challenges they faced in their pursuit.

Theo listened intently, nodding as he absorbed the information.

"We will now make calls once a week, as we are traveling to Maharashtra.

We have received information about the train," Celia interjected, her voice brightening the conversation.

"But why were you unable to call us during the day?" Selena inquired, her tone reflecting a shared sense of urgency.

"It is the same for us; we wake up early to seek clues," Damien added, his voice steady and determined.

The conversation flowed, filled with ideas and theories, as they brainstormed their next steps. They discussed the various leads they had gathered, each one more intriguing than the last.

However, just as the discussion reached a pivotal point,

Theo's phone suddenly lost power, leaving the conversation unfinished and the group in a state of uncertainty.

After a brief moment of silence, Dilen picked up a book that had been lying on the table.

As he flipped through the pages, an idea struck him.

"While perusing the book, we realized we could also investigate the motorman currently operating that train," he suggested, his eyes lighting up with inspiration.

The group quickly shifted their focus to the motorman, researching to uncover any information they could find.

After some digging, they discovered that a man named Lucan had been on that train, but he had exited for reasons that remained shrouded in mystery.

"Some speculate that he intended to commit suicide," Dilen said, his voice low, "but that is untrue; he was attempting to save himself

They just estimate because nobody knows the reality.

I can say that nobody has proof.

On the website, it was written that he used to live in Amritsar but he left his house and transferred to Daman.

26

Meeting Lucan- the train engineer

The sky outside had taken on a strange, bruised hue—deep grey laced with streaks of violet, as though the day were ending and beginning at the same time. The light was dim but not quite night, an in-between shade that flattened the land into muted shapes.

The ground on either side of the tracks was rough and uneven, dotted with clusters of blackened stones and patches of dry grass that swayed without any wind to move them.

The train's wheels carried on their steady rhythm, though it felt slower now, each turn dragging slightly before catching pace again. From somewhere beneath the carriage came a dull, intermittent knock, faint but persistent, as if something loose had been shaken into life by the miles.

Inside, the air was cool, laced with the faint smell of damp metal. The lamps burned low, their glow warm but dim, pooling in uneven shapes on the floor. The aisle seemed longer than before, stretching into a haze at the far end, where the outline of the next compartment door stood in shadow.

The luggage racks overhead were empty save for one lone strap that swayed gently, tapping in a slow, steady rhythm against the rail.

Through the window, shapes began to appear in the distance—tall, thin structures that might have been towers, or perhaps the remains of something older. They loomed for only moments before the train swept past, leaving behind the unsettling certainty that they had been closer than they appeared.

Somewhere deep in the train, a door closed with deliberate force. The sound carried down the corridor, resonating in the quiet before being swallowed by the hum of the wheels. It felt like a signal, though of what, no one could yet tell.

We traveled to his residence, conveniently located just a mile from the hotel.

The short drive was filled with anticipation, and after a brief journey, we arrived at his home.

To our pleasant surprise, the interior was immaculate, a level of cleanliness we hadn't anticipated given the busy schedules we knew he kept.

The living room was tidy, with everything in its place, and the faint scent of fresh linen lingered in the air.

Although he might be traveling in the future, the tidiness of his home was impressive and spoke volumes about his attention to detail.

At that moment, Nilen remarked that it was likely his wife maintained the house regularly, a thought that seemed to resonate with all of us.

It was clear that someone took great care in ensuring their home was welcoming and orderly.

"Forget about that, let's head inside," Dacy suggested, eager to get to the matter at hand.

We approached the door and pressed the doorbell, the chime echoing softly through the house. Almost immediately, his wife greeted us with a warm smile, saying, "Hello! What brings you here?" Her friendly demeanor put us at ease, and we felt welcomed right away.

Caleb stepped forward, responding, "We need to speak with Lucan; we have some matters to discuss."

She nodded understandingly and welcomed us in, gesturing for us to take a seat in the cozy living room.

She then called for Lucan, her voice carrying a hint of excitement as she announced our arrival.

"Yes, how can I assist you?" Lucan asked as he entered the room, his expression shifting from curiosity to attentiveness.

We wasted no time and inquired about train 331, sharing our detailed account of the situation that had been troubling us.

We explained the delays, the confusion surrounding the schedules, and the impact it had on our plans.

"Oh, so you're experiencing the same issues," Lucan replied, his brow furrowing in understanding.

"I've also faced a lot of difficulties because of that train."

His empathy was evident, and it was clear that he was not just a bystander in this situation; he had been affected by it as well.

"Let's collaborate," he proposed, his tone shifting to one of determination.

"If we pool our resources and information, we might be able to find a solution or at least make our voices heard."

"We would be happy to," Dilen agreed enthusiastically, his eyes lighting up at the prospect of working together.

Lucan recounted the entire incident with a heavy heart, his voice tinged with the weight of memories that refused to fade.

"On that fateful day," he began, "I was on the train, just another routine journey when a group of robbers stormed in.

It was chaos—gunfire erupted, and in an instant, lives were lost.

Everyone except for a few who remained silent, who perhaps understood the gravity of the situation, fell victim to the violence.

I realized something was amiss when I heard the first shots ring out, sharp and jarring against the hum of the train.

I turned to my partner, desperate to alert them, but they dismissed my concerns, believing it was just the train noise or perhaps a loudspeaker being used by rowdy passengers.

Lucan's eyes darkened as he continued, "As the noise escalated, we felt a primal instinct kick in. Sensing the danger closing in, I made a split-second decision. We leaped from the train just as the criminals entered the cabin, their faces twisted with malice.

Thankfully, we managed to escape, but the horror of that day haunted me.

My partner, still oblivious to the reality of the situation, thought it was all just a misunderstanding.

After that, I lost track of what transpired inside the train. I could only imagine the chaos that unfolded."

Her brow furrowed in concern, Emily inquired about the women's voices that had been echoing in their discussions.

Lucan paused, uncertainty flickering across his face.

"I'm not sure," he admitted, his voice barely above a whisper.

Damien, ever the analytical one, chimed in, "Some of those voices are from 2018, while others seem to be present now.

We were separated, and it's hard to piece it all together."

Peter, who had been quietly listening, interjected with a sense of urgency.

"We possess a diary known as the future book, which accurately predicts future dates. It's a crucial piece of the puzzle."

Lucan nodded, his mind racing with possibilities. He then pointed to a picture of the train's entry book displayed on the wall.

"This book contains information about the train that only I know.

If we place this book in the designated port, the train will operate according to the engineers' specifications.

We have discovered one diary—the future book—but we still need to locate the second and third diaries, which pertain to the past and the overall timeline.

Wait! Why don't we go to the railway station and ask one of the staff who worked when Lucan was in charge of the train with his partner, said Emily.

It's a good idea, said Damien.

Sorry everyone but tomorrow I am going to the USA to visit my friend, but I will come within a month meanwhile you all try to find the clues related, replied Lucan.

After a month

Did you all manage to find the clues, questioned Lucan; no, we tried to, but couldn't, said Nilen.

Okay, okay, so let's go to the railway station today at 5:30 to find out more information about that train, said Lucan.

27

Nilen's sacrifice

The outside world had fallen into an eerie stillness, as though the landscape itself were holding its breath. The sky was a solid sheet of dark steel, without sun, moon, or star, the horizon blending seamlessly into the land. The fields on either side were empty and bare, stretching away into a haze that seemed to swallow distance itself.

No movement stirred—no birds, no wind, only the unbroken line of the tracks vanishing into the gloom ahead.

The train's wheels rolled on, their sound muted, almost swallowed by the silence beyond the glass.

A faint vibration shivered through the floor, but the usual creaks and groans of the carriage were absent, leaving an unnatural quiet between each turn of the rails. Every so often, the faint echo of something—like a distant metallic tap—drifted along the corridor, though no source could be seen.

Inside, the lamps glowed faintly, casting long, soft shadows across the aisle. The seats stood in perfect order, untouched, their fabric catching the light in dull ripples as the train swayed. A thin draft slid through an unseen gap, cold against the skin, carrying with it a faint scent of wet stone and something older—something that didn't belong to the journey.

Through the window, a shape emerged in the distance—tall, narrow, unmoving. At first it seemed like another signal post, but as the train drew closer, it revealed no markings, no wires, only a smooth, dark silhouette. The moment the train passed it, the air inside seemed to grow heavier, as though whatever it was had noticed.

The tracks ahead vanished into a stretch of deepening shadow, and with it came the unshakable feeling that the journey was not heading toward an end, but toward something waiting in the dark.

At 5:30 pm, the sun began to dip below the horizon, casting a warm golden hue over the streets.

We found ourselves on the route to the railway station, our excitement palpable.

However, our journey took an unexpected turn when our car suffered a punctured tire, leading to the vehicle's stop.

The sudden jolt and the subsequent realization that we were stranded left us with no choice but to abandon the vehicle.

We walked the remaining distance to the station, which was nearby.

As we made our way along the bustling road, the sounds of the city enveloped us—the honking of the horns, the chatter of pedestrians, and the distant rumble of trains. It was then that Nilen's attention was drawn to a small boy, no older than six, who was attempting to cross the road.

The child, with his innocent eyes and carefree demeanor, seemed blissfully unaware of the danger that loomed him just a few feet away.

A truck, barreling down the street at an alarming speed, was hurtling towards him, and time seemed to slow down as Nilen's heart raced loudly.

In that instant, a flood of memories washed over Nilen, transporting him back to his childhood. He recalled a fateful day when he had been in a similar predicament, a day that had forever altered the course of his life.

He had been the small boy, oblivious to the approaching danger when a brave soul—another boy, perhaps just a year or two older—had risked everything to save him. Nilen's heart ached as he remembered the sacrifice that had been made that day.

Although he had survived, the boy who had thrown himself into harm's way had tragically lost his life in the process. Overcome with emotion, Nilen's eyes filled with tears as he reflected on the themes of sacrifice and selflessness that had defined that moment.

The memory of the brave boy's last words echoed in his mind: "If it is God's will, it will so happen." Those words, spoken with a mix of courage and resignation, had stayed with Nilen throughout the years, a haunting reminder of the fragility of life and the profound impact of one person's bravery.

Without a second thought for his safety, Nilen sprang into action, propelled by a deep-seated instinct to protect the innocent child before him. He dashed into the street, his heart pounding in his chest, as he reached out to grab the boy just in time.

Impact description

The journey had become quieter than ever. The hum of the wheels, once steady and reassuring, now carried an uneven depth—each metallic note ringing longer than it should, as if the sound were echoing through something vast and hollow. The usual sway of the carriage was still there, but the air felt different. Heavier. Thicker.

Beyond the glass, the world had shed all signs of life. The last faint glimmer of a settlement had faded hours ago, replaced by an unbroken stretch of muted land and a sky without light. No moon. No stars. Just a solid blanket of darkness, the kind that swallows everything it touches. The horizon was gone; the earth simply faded into the void, leaving the sense that the train might be floating rather than moving on rails.

Inside, the lamps flickered intermittently, never settling into a constant glow. Thcy would flarc bricfly, revealing the worn upholstery, the faint scuffs along the aisle, the empty luggage racks… and then dim again, letting the shadows reclaim every surface. When the light failed, the space seemed to stretch—rows of seats appearing to pull farther apart, the ceiling seeming higher, the aisle narrowing into a tunnel of black.

Somewhere far down the corridor, a faint sound tapped against the floor—a slow, deliberate rhythm that didn't match the train's motion. Tap… pause… tap… pause… as though something was pacing. It stopped each time the lamps brightened, then resumed the instant they dimmed.

The passengers had grown unnervingly still. A man near the front sat with his head turned toward the window, unmoving. A woman in the middle carriage gripped the edge of her seat, her knuckles white, eyes fixed on the aisle as though waiting for something to appear. And yet, no one spoke. Words seemed dangerous here.

Outside, a shape began to form in the distance—a tall, narrow silhouette standing alone beside the tracks. At first it seemed like a signal post, but its proportions were wrong. It was too thin. Too smooth. It had no markings, no wires, nothing to tie it to the railway. The train moved closer, and for a brief, unshakable moment, it seemed to turn—not physically, but in the way a shadow shifts when light changes direction—aligning itself toward the carriage as if noticing them.

The moment the train passed it, every lamp inside flickered wildly, casting the shadows into chaotic motion. The tapping sound down the corridor stopped. A breathless stillness filled the air, the kind that comes just before something happens.

Then the lights went out completely.

The darkness was absolute, swallowing even the reflection of the windows. Only the sound of the wheels remained—but even that was changing, the pitch dipping lower, the intervals between each clatter stretching farther apart. It felt as though the train had left its rails entirely, continuing forward on a path that no one could see.

Somewhere ahead, faint lights began to appear. They weren't the warm, welcoming glow of a station. They were cold, steady, and pulsing faintly, each one separated by long stretches of black. The rhythm of their pulse was slow… deliberate… almost alive.

The passengers did not move. The air inside felt charged, as though the train were passing through something unseen, something that could feel them as much as they could feel it. The pulse of the lights grew stronger. The wheels struck something hollow. And from somewhere far ahead in the dark, a sound rose—deep, resonant, and impossible to place, neither human nor machine.

It came once.
It came again, closer.

And then—

"…we realized the journey had never been about where we were going, but about what had been waiting for us to arrive."

What would be their reaction? what would be their feelings about Nilen? Is he dead? what will they do now? What will they tell the group who are in 2018? What will become of his? What do you think will happen with Nilen? what will be the next? What step will they take? Find it out in 2nd part.

Quotes (by Alden Dalmet)

"Sometimes the past doesn't stay behind,it boards the train with you."

If life takes you away from your family,

Face the obstacle and change the fate of your life.

No matter how long you would face,

But never lose hope of meeting your family again.

Some journeys end at the last stop,

But some begin only after the last stop

Contact/ Follow Me

Instagram: @alden_331

Facebook: Alden Dalmet

Email: aldendalmet@gmail.com or aldendalmet331@gmail.com
Feel free to send feedback, questions, and queries, and if you find what should be added or what shouldn't, contact me
Snapchat: Alden Dalmet
Signal: 7744803200

Contact: 8390379084

WhatsApp: 7875370661, Alden Dalmet

YouTube Channel: Alden Dalmet
I upload songs here — if you like my music, please like, share, and subscribe to support my channel and write your thoughts in the comments.

To be continued in part 2 …

Thank you for reading

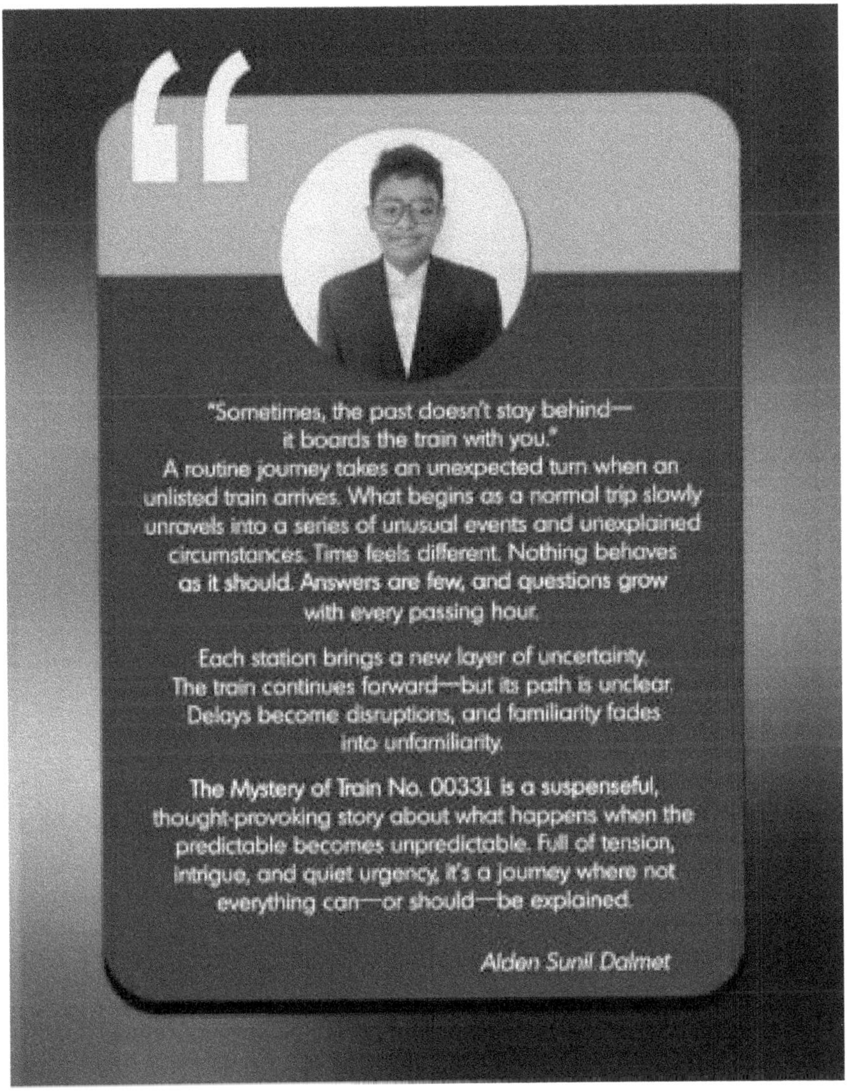
"Sometimes, the past doesn't stay behind—
it boards the train with you."
A routine journey takes an unexpected turn when an unlisted train arrives. What begins as a normal trip slowly unravels into a series of unusual events and unexplained circumstances. Time feels different. Nothing behaves as it should. Answers are few, and questions grow with every passing hour.
Each station brings a new layer of uncertainty. The train continues forward—but its path is unclear. Delays become disruptions, and familiarity fades into unfamiliarity.
The Mystery of Train No. 00331 is a suspenseful, thought-provoking story about what happens when the predictable becomes unpredictable. Full of tension, intrigue, and quiet urgency, it's a journey where not everything can—or should—be explained.
Alden Sunil Dalmet

www.ingramcontent.com/pod-product-compliance
Ingram Content Group UK Ltd.
Pitfield, Milton Keynes, MK11 3LW, UK
UKHW021344190726
13845UKWH00027B/714

9 789334 366761